The Volk

OrangeBooks Publication

1st Floor, Rajhans Arcade, Mall Road, Kohka, Bhilai, Chhattisgarh 490020

Website: **www.orangebooks.in**

First Edition, 2025

ISBN: 978-93-6554-903-4

Price: Rs. 350.00

Printed in India

THE VOLK

A PAST FORGOTTEN

SAHIL CHOUDHARY

OrangeBooks Publication
www.orangebooks.in

Author's Note

Welcome to The Volk Universe.

This is the first part of a story planned to span four editions at least, each one building upon the last and revealing more of the enigmatic character of Volk. My aim with this book was to create a narrative that feels like it's already unfolding on the big screen. I'm hopeful that I'll connect with some of my favorite directors who can do justice to the story. If you can share this book within your network, that would mean a lot.

Written in a screenplay-inspired format, the pacing is intentionally quick, with some sections shorter than you might expect from a traditional novel. It's my attempt to offer a fresh experience for modern readers—those who are constantly on the move, exploring stories but often don't have time for lengthy books that stretch on forever. It's a break from the endless stream of YouTube and online content that can leave the mind drained. I hope this format is adopted in the future—maybe we should call it "Scrovel"—a fusion of screenplay and novel.

I was initially told to write it as a novella, but that approach left me with a story that lacked energy and charm. And after 6-8 months of experimenting with different styles, I decided on this format. While new ideas are often met with resistance, I chose to self-publish rather than chase publishers and agents for months, maybe years. The story needed to be out there for the amazing readers and artists who are constantly looking for new, exciting stories.

You might find moments where the rhythm feels unconventional for traditional readers. There will be places where the story jumps quickly from scene to scene, almost like watching a film. This isn't an oversight; it's a deliberate choice to keep the storytelling tight, focused, and immersive. If you approach the book as it is, I believe you'll enjoy it as a new style of storytelling—one that bridges novels and screenplays in a way that reflects how we consume stories today.

This is my first attempt at blending these styles, and your feedback will help shape how "The Volk" evolves in future editions—and maybe even help establish this genre, Scrovel. I'm excited for you to be part of this journey and look forward to hearing your thoughts. Use Hashtag **#TheVolkUniverse** if you intend to talk about this book anywhere online.

For feedback, please email me to below mentioned email with the subject "The Volk Feedback," and I'll be happy to consider your input for the next prints and editions.

— Sahil Choudhary

Email: sahil.pedazo@gmail.com

Acknowledgments

I'd like to extend my heartfelt gratitude to everyone who helped me bring this story to life:

Firstly, to my soulmate, Sheena, whose constant encouragement led me to write this book. I often share my weird and imaginative dreams with her, and one day, after hearing yet another wild story, she smiled and said, "This sounds like a movie'. That simple comment lit the spark that became this story. To my friend, Magistrate Adnan Naqshbandi, who inspired me to envision it as a screenplay for a TV series and could already see it as a Studio Ghibli anime unfolding before his eyes. And to so many other friends who have contributed to the book—your invaluable guidance and encouragement have meant the world to me.

I also want to thank Ebraheem Al Jarrah for the Arabic dialogue translations ensuring the authenticity of the story. To add further authenticity, I personally traveled to Kashmir and Ladakh during the writing process to immerse myself in the landscape and engage with locals for inspiration.

Finally, I'd like to thank my dear friend Mohammad Shahzaan Rahi, who helped with the ladakhi and kashmiri translations.

Without your support, this book would not have been possible.

Thank you for being part of this journey.

— **Sahil Choudhary**

Contents

The Frozen Expanse

Amelia's breath came in short, painful bursts, her leg twisted grotesquely beneath her. Snow stung like needles, blanketing everything in sight, stretching far beyond the horizon, as if the world itself were wrapped in a pale, icy shroud. Endless, pristine whiteness dominated the Siberian wilderness, disrupted only by the rhythmic fall of fresh flakes that descended heavily, almost relentlessly, from a sky that seemed both oppressive and infinite. Bitter winds tore through the open plains, creating a haunting symphony, as if the land itself were alive and warning them to leave.

It was midday, though the sun, shrouded by thick clouds, offered little warmth or comfort. The cold gnawed at exposed skin, seeping deep into bones, and even the thickest layers seemed powerless against it. In the distance, the howls of unseen dogs echoed, faint but ominous, carried across the snow like ghostly calls. The sound only heightened the isolation, an eerie reminder of the predators lurking somewhere within the vast, unforgiving expanse.

Behind a towering, snow-crusted glacier, three figures crouched together in a pitiful huddle, the bitter cold and exhaustion visible in every line of their bodies. Amelia sat between Khalid and Jason, shivering violently. Her usually lively eyes were clouded with fear, her face pale and streaked with dirt, the color drained from her lips. She clutched her leg, which lay twisted at an unnatural angle, grimacing in pain as she struggled to control her labored breaths.

"We... we should have listened. We shouldn't have come here," Amelia whispered, her voice barely audible

against the howling wind. Regret was etched into every word, her defiance from earlier now, a distant memory overshadowed by a harsh, chilling reality.

The sharp, biting cold did nothing to dull the memory that rose unbidden in her mind. Amelia closed her eyes, and in an instant, she was no longer in the frozen wasteland of Siberia but standing in her father's grand study, where warmth and opulence contrasted sharply with her current predicament.

***

The air in the study had been heavy with the scent of leather and oak, mingling with a faint whiff of smoke from the crackling fireplace. Mahogany shelves lined the walls, filled with meticulously arranged leather-bound volumes that reflected her father's disciplined, traditional taste. Warm golden light bathed the room, casting a soft glow over the dark wood and creating an almost reverent atmosphere. Yet the warmth of the room could do nothing to soothe the cold, unforgiving glare her father fixed upon her.

Her father, a powerful man in his late forties, was a figure who rarely softened, his presence demanding respect and fear in equal measure. His face was set in a hard frown, and he looked at her with an expression that was half disappointment, half frustration.

He stood beside the fireplace, arms crossed, the flickering light casting shadows across his stern features.

"Amelia, you don't just get away from your life," he said, his voice calm but edged with an unyielding firmness.

"Running off to Siberia isn't a game—it's reckless."

Amelia squared her shoulders, her jaw set in defiance.

"Maybe to you, it's reckless. But to me, it's freedom," she shot back, meeting his gaze with a fierce determination.

"I don't want to be chained to this house or your plans for me."

Her words hung heavily in the air, clashing with the quiet crackling of the fire. Her father's jaw tightened, a clear sign of his irritation, yet he remained silent, scrutinizing her as though searching for a glimmer of doubt in her eyes.

"And what's freedom to you?", he retorted; his voice now tinged with exasperation.

"Gallivanting off to the end of the Earth with no thought of what might happen to you?"

Amelia felt her frustration bubbling over, her fists clenched at her sides.

"I'll be with Khalid and Jason," she insisted, willing herself to keep her voice steady.

"They understand me. They don't try to control me. For once, I need to make my own choices. Please, Dad."

Just then, the soft creak of a door interrupted their argument, and both turned to see Amelia's stepmother standing quietly in the doorway. Her calm, gentle presence seemed to diffuse some of the tension in the room.

In her mid-thirties, she carried an effortless elegance and warmth that softened the sharpness of the room. Moving to her husband's side, she placed a hand on his arm, her gaze soft but resolute.

"Let her go, darling," she murmured, her voice soothing.

"She's not a little girl anymore. Maybe this will teach her things we can't."

Father (grudgingly):

"And when something goes wrong, who do you think will have to deal with it?"

Stepmother (whispering, encouraging):

"She's young. She needs to find her path. We can't shelter her forever."

Amelia watches, her face softening as her stepmother speaks up in her defense. She steps forward, her tone more vulnerable.

Amelia, *"Please, just trust me. I need this... just to be away from all of this for a little while."*

The father looked between his wife and Amelia, his expression wavered for a moment, the hard lines of his face softening slightly as he considered his wife's words. He sighed, rubbing his forehead as though weary of the battle. He turned back to Amelia, his face shadowed with a reluctant acceptance.

"Fine," he said at last, his tone was heavy with resignation.

"But remember, Amelia—you chose this. Don't expect me to come running when you realize how unforgiving the world can be."

Amelia nodded, her face, a mixture of gratitude and defiance, a silent promise that she would prove him wrong. With one last look at her father, she'd turned and left the room, the weight of her decision settling heavily on her shoulders as she stepped into the unknown.

***

Back in the present, huddled against the glacier with the relentless wind tearing through her clothing, Amelia's father's words echoed in her mind. She shuddered, not just from the cold but from the haunting realization of how right he had been. She had wanted freedom.

Now, freedom felt like punishment. She looked at Jason and Khalid's troubled faces, and a sudden image flickered behind her eyelids—another memory, vivid and sharp, pulling Amelia back to a different place and time...

***

Amelia sat cross-legged on her bed; her room dimly lit except for the soft glow of her laptop screen. The excitement bubbling inside her felt almost surreal. She stared at her reflection on the screen for a moment, taking a deep breath as she clicked on the video call. Her friends' faces began to appear one by one, each in a setting as unique as their personalities.

The first was Khalid. His camera revealed a room so lavish it could have belonged to royalty, complete with grand arches, gilded decor, and the soft, luxurious lighting of a palace. And there, in the background, lay a tiger—casually sprawled across a plush cushion. Khalid himself looked effortlessly poised, wearing traditional Arab robes that draped elegantly around him, his expression sharp but calm, as if the sight of a tiger lounging nearby was nothing out of the ordinary.

Amelia couldn't help but laugh, the image both startling and hilarious. Just as she was about to comment, Jason's face popped up, a huge grin plastered across it. He wore a pair of aviator sunglasses, clearly enjoying the sun-drenched beach behind him. The endless stretch of golden sand and sparkling ocean gave his backdrop a carefree energy that contrasted sharply with Khalid's palace.

And finally, Elly joined the call. Her setting was polished and sophisticated, reflecting her meticulous nature. Her sleek, modern bedroom was adorned with framed awards, each testament to her ambition and dedication. Designer handbags and luxury fashion pieces were neatly displayed, a subtle showcase of her success.

Amelia's grin widened as she took in the sight of her friends, each so different yet each integral to the group. She leaned closer to the screen, her eyes shining with excitement.

"Guys! I finally convinced my dad! We're going!"

Khalid smirked, leaning back with a self-assured ease.

"Of course you did. Welcome to the team, Amelia. I wouldn't let anything stand in the way of this trip."

He snapped his fingers, and the tiger in the background lazily lifted its head, its large, amber eyes casting a sleepy glance toward the screen.

The reaction was instant; Amelia's startled expression made everyone burst into laughter, the sound carrying warmth and camaraderie through the screen.

Jason shook his head, laughing.

"Only Khalid would casually have a tiger as a house pet. Man, you're living a whole other life."

Khalid chuckled, glancing over his shoulder at the majestic creature.

"One must have the proper companions, right? And speaking of companions, I've arranged everything for our little adventure."

Elly leaned forward, her eyes glinting with intrigue.

"Ooh, details please! You've been so secretive about this."

Khalid flashed a mysterious smile.

"I wanted it to be a surprise. But alright, I'll give you a hint. Remember the statue of Togo, we saw during our last trip to Alaska?"

Amelia's mind raced, recalling the tale of Leonhard Seppala's historic journey through the Alaskan wilderness, led by his loyal dog Togo in a race against time to save lives. It was a story of resilience, of unbreakable bonds and bravery. Khalid's excitement was contagious, and she found herself leaning in closer, drawn to his words.

Khalid continued, his voice laced with excitement.

"I found a location in Siberia with a similar vibe. It's wild, untouched—perfect for what we're after. Imagine snow-covered landscapes, frozen lakes, towering ice cliffs. It'll be breathtaking, and the weather's set to be harsh but beautiful. Exactly what I wanted."

He leaned back, his expression proud and pleased, as though he'd just unveiled a masterpiece.

Jason's eyebrows shot up; his usual grin replaced by a look of genuine awe.

"Bro, that sounds insane. But are you sure we're ready for Siberia? That's next-level cold. We're not exactly survival experts."

Khalid's smirk only grew, his confidence unwavering.

"Don't worry. I've hired a professional team and security who knows the terrain. They'll be around to guide us, but we'll have our privacy. And yes, we'll have the best equipment money can buy. Imagine it—a private documentary capturing every moment, every challenge, every thrill."

Amelia's heart raced.

"Wait, we're filming it all? Like a real documentary?"

Khalid nodded, his eyes glinting with excitement.

"Absolutely. They'll document everything—from the biting cold to the thrill of conquering nature. This won't just be another trip. It'll be the ultimate test of endurance, a memory we'll carry forever."

Elly clapped her hands, her laughter bright and carefree.

"This is way more exciting than I imagined! It'll be epic. My dad would freak if he knew, but I've been dreaming of something like this forever."

Jason leaned forward, his grin returning.

"Yeah, this is exactly the kind of story that'll get people talking. 'So, what did you do over break?' 'Oh, you know, just survived Siberia!'"

Khalid raised a glass, a mock toast to the adventure they were about to undertake.

"To adventure, to pushing limits, and to Siberia. This is going to be legendary."

They clinked their imaginary glasses on the screen, laughter and excitement filling the air. For a moment, each of them sat in silence, letting the magnitude of the adventure sink in. This was more than just a trip; it was a declaration of independence, of defiance against the comfortable lives they each left behind. And now, for better or worse, they were in it together.

***

Back in present, the snow-covered wilderness stretched as far as the eye could see, an endless expanse of pristine white, broken only by the jagged outline of a distant glacier. The wind cut like a blade, whistling through the

Siberian plains, and the cold crept deep, past layers of clothing, numbing everything it touched. Beneath a sky of steel-gray clouds, three figures huddled close, their faces pale, breaths fogging the frigid air.

Khalid, his voice low and urgent, leaned close to Amelia,

"Stay calm. We just... we need to stay quiet."

His tone was steady, but his eyes betrayed the fear gnawing at him.

Beside him, Jason clutched his ribs, his hand trembling as blood seeped between his fingers. He glanced at Khalid, panic flickering in his gaze.

"You said it would be a thrill, right? A thrill...," he whispered, his voice barely audible, the words tinged with bitterness and fear.

Then, a sound—low and menacing—broke the silence. A growl rolled through the air, freezing them in place. Slowly, their eyes turned toward the shadows cast by the glacier's towering form. Out of the dim light, a massive shape emerged, moving with a predator's grace. The hulking figure of a Siberian tiger prowled toward them, its golden eyes locked onto them, glinting with a deadly focus. Blood streaked its fur, a grim reminder of its recent kill—Elly, their companion, who lay motionless in the snow just a few yards away, her lifeless eyes staring blankly into the endless sky.

Amelia caught sight of her fallen friend, a strangled sob escaping her lips.

"That should have been me," she whispered, looking away, her voice cracking with regret and despair.

"I should have been her..."

Khalid placed a trembling hand on her shoulder, trying to ground them both.

"Shhh... stay quiet," he murmured, his voice thick with tension.

"Tigers... they don't hunt humans unless provoked. We just need to stay hidden."

But Jason's breathing grew louder, shallow and panicked, each gasp a frantic exclamation. The tiger's ears perked up, and it lifted its head, nostrils flaring as it caught the scent of Jason's blood.

"We're dead," Jason whispered frantically, his voice cracking.

"We're dead, Khalid. We can't fight this thing... we must run—"

Khalid shot him a furious look, his voice a harsh whisper,

"Jason, shut up! You'll get us all killed."

The tiger's growl deepened, and it took a slow, deliberate step forward. Amelia held her breath, the terror freezing her in place. Her mind raced, prayers and pleas colliding in her thoughts. Jason, in his panic, finally lost control. Ignoring Khalid's warnings, he bolted, stumbling through the snow in a desperate attempt to escape.

"Jason, stop! Don't—"

Khalid began, but his words fell into silence as the tiger lunged. With terrifying speed, the beast closed the distance and pounced, slamming Jason to the ground. Jason cried out in agony, struggling beneath the weight of the creature.

Khalid sprang to his feet, shouting desperately.

"Hey! Over here! Come on, you beast, look at me!"

Amelia watched, her heart pounding, as Khalid tried to draw the tiger's attention, his face set in determination.

"Stay behind me," he said, his voice steady.

"I'll hold it off."

But Amelia barely hears him. Her ankle throbs painfully as she struggles to stand, her mind racing. With a terrifying roar, the tiger lunges forward. Khalid thrusts his stick forward, aiming for its eyes in a desperate last attempt to protect them. But the beast swats it aside with brutal strength, sending Khalid sprawling backward into the snow. He clutches his arm, blood pouring down as he tries to steady himself, forcing himself onto his knees.

Khalid (gasping, voice choked): *"Amelia... run."*

Amelia fights to stand, desperation driving her to push through the searing pain in her twisted ankle. But just as she gains her footing, her strength gives way, and she collapses into the snow with a painful cry, clutching her leg. The tiger's cold, ruthless gaze shifts to her, and she feels her blood run cold. She was helpless, vulnerable, with no escape.

The tiger's shadow loomed over her, each step bringing it closer. Amelia's heart hammered, her breaths shallow and quick. She squeezed her eyes shut, whispering a desperate prayer.

Suddenly, a sharp whistle cuts through the frozen silence, catching the tiger's attention. The beast freezes, its nostrils flaring in alarm. An arrow slices through the air, missing the tiger and tearing through its side. It snarls in pain, a thin line of blood trickling down its matted fur, but instead of retreating, it seems only more enraged.

Amelia's eyes flew open, and she looked around, her heart leaping with hope. Across the clearing, a dark figure emerged from the snow—a man, tall and rugged, his eyes as cold as the Siberian wilderness itself. He lowered his bow, sliding it back over his shoulder, then drew two gleaming katanas from his back. Their silver edges caught the faint light, a stark contrast against the shadows of the snow.

The tiger released a feral growl, its gaze locking onto this new threat. It lowered itself, muscles coiling as it prepared to strike.

The man held his ground, unmoved, his stance calm and unwavering. With one last snarl, the tiger leaped, its massive form hurtling through the air. But the man was faster. He sidestepped with practiced ease, his blades flashing in a deadly arc. The steel sliced cleanly through the tiger's throat, blood spraying into the air, a vivid red against the white snow, as the beast's head separates from its body.

The tiger's body collapsed, and Amelia felt its weight press down on her as it pinned her beneath it. She gasped, her face splattered with blood, her vision blurring, as shock and exhaustion overtook her. The last thing she saw before darkness claimed her was the stranger's silhouette, his katanas dripping red against the white expanse, his gaze as cold and unyielding as the Siberian night.

***

The night settled over the frozen lake, a sheet of dark indigo stretched above the Siberian wilderness, stars sparkling like scattered diamonds. Across the ice, a sledge carved a swift path, the only movement in this vast, desolate expanse. The sledge, pulled by a team of huskies, seemed almost ghostly in the silence. At the head of the pack ran a white wolf, Yuki, guiding the way with instinctive purpose, while a black wolf, Zeus, followed closely behind, a silent sentinel watching over their fragile cargo.

In the front of the sledge, Amelia lay unconscious, her face as pale as the snow beneath her. Blood streaked across her cheek, a chilling reminder of the recent tiger attack that had nearly claimed her life. Next to her, Khalid sat slumped, clutching his shoulder. He felt the warmth of his blood seeping through his makeshift bandage but held himself upright, enduring the pain with grim resilience. Jason lay nearby, his breaths shallow, the pain etched across his face as he hovered on the edge of consciousness. They were alive, but just barely.

At the back of the sledge, a man steered with calm determination, his expression unreadable, his gaze steady as he scanned the icy horizon. His shoulders draped in a fresh tiger pelt, its fur still matted with blood that glistened in the moonlight, a testament to the violence of their encounter. A cigar smoldered between his lips as he exhaled a steady stream of smoke, the tendrils curling into the frigid air, mingling with the frost and adding to his shadowed, enigmatic presence.

The image of this man—stoic and relentless—sharp and defined, his abs chiseled, outlined by the soft glow of the moon. His medium-length, straight hair fluttered in the wind, revealing a demeanor of calm and resolve, almost otherworldly against the stark backdrop of night. He steered the sledge with the confidence of someone who knew exactly what needed to be done. To an outsider, his image might have been haunting, but here, he was simply survival incarnate.

They surged forward, and with each bump of the sledge, fragments of Jason's memories clawed their way to the surface. He saw it again—the tiger emerging like a specter from the shadows, its amber eyes fixed on them. He remembered his own voice, rough with fear, shouting for help. In his memory, Jason saw this man arrive.

***

The sledge moved across the frozen lake; the huskies looked aggressive, and the bodies of the crew lay lifeless on the ice. The scene was chaotic, a blur of snow and shadows as the remnants of their confrontation with the tiger lingered in the air.

Jason (breathless, desperation etched on his face): *"Help... please. My friends—they're still out there!"*

The man, silent and unreadable, moved with purpose, his heavy boots crunching against the snow as he strode across the icy terrain. His eyes scanned the surroundings with the keen precision of a predator. He located Amelia, pinned beneath the massive frame of the tiger, her pale skin contrasting sharply with the vibrant blood.

Without hesitation, the man stepped forward. In one fluid motion, he fired an arrow at the tiger. Moments later, its head rolled away into the snow with a soft thud, and its body collapsed lifelessly onto Amelia. With a single, decisive movement, he lifted Amelia effortlessly, cradling her in his strong arms. He laid her on the sledge and wrapped her in his Coat with the utmost care, shielding her from the icy wind.

Jason, bleeding heavily, clung weakly to Khalid, his face contorted in pain, barely conscious but desperate to help. The man's demeanor shifted slightly as he assessed their dire situation. He removed his undershirt, torn and stained, and quickly tore it into strips. With grim efficiency, he placed a piece in Jason's mouth.

Man (coolly, maintaining eye contact with Khalid):

"Hold him down."

Khalid nodded, despite the pain coursing through his own body. He gripped Jason's shoulders tightly, trying to keep him steady as the man prepared to address the wounds. The man poured around half a bottle of alcohol onto the bleeding gash in Jason's side, the pungent liquid spilling over the raw flesh. Jason cried out, the sound a mix of pain and shock as the alcohol stung like fire.

Man (unmoved, his tone flat):

"Scream."

Jason's protests faded into weak whimpers as the man tightened the makeshift bandages, wrapping them around Jason's body with the practiced hands of someone well-versed in survival. Each twist of the fabric elicited small gasps from Jason, who teetered on the brink of consciousness.

He was now bare-chested, having stripped away all his upper clothing to tend to Jason's wounds. The harsh Siberian cold bit into his exposed skin, but instead of weakening him, it seemed to sharpen every contour of his body. His muscles were carved and defined — abs harder than ice itself, each ridge and hollow accentuated by the biting wind. The cold air clung to his skin, making the taut planes of his torso look almost sculpted, as if nature itself had forged him from frozen stone. Despite the brutal environment, there was an undeniable strength and resilience radiating from him, silent proof that he was built for survival in these unforgiving lands.

Finally, the man turned back to the tiger, his gaze sharp and calculating. He unsheathed his large hunting knife, the blade gleaming ominously in the dim light. He began to skin the animal with deliberate precision, each cut almost ritualistic. The thick fur fell away in strips, revealing the raw muscle beneath, which glistened in the fading twilight.

The blood from the carcass seeped into the snow, spreading in slow, winding rivulets that mirrored the veins of some great dying beast. Steam still rose from the tiger's body, curling upward and vanishing into the twilight like the ghost of the predator it once was. He didn't flinch at the sight, nor at the copper tang of blood that clung to the air. His hands, stained and shaking slightly from exertion, continued their work with a mechanical calm, as though skinning wild beasts were a task no more foreign than tying shoelaces. It wasn't cruelty—it was necessity. He had done worse in colder places, with less reason.

As the fur was peeled away, the man draped it across his shoulders—not as a trophy, but as a necessity forged in desperation. The tiger's warmth, still clinging to the freshly severed hide, wrapped around him like a crude shield against the elements. He had surrendered his coat to Amelia earlier, without hesitation, knowing the cold would bite deep into her fragile frame. Jason, barely conscious, was swaddled in what little remained of the man's own clothing. There was no valor in his sacrifice—only instinct, shaped by years of hardship, honed through encounters where hesitation meant death. The hide wasn't a symbol of triumph. It was armor, camouflage, and warmth, all in one—his only chance to keep moving forward.

With the tiger's hide secured, the man returned to the sledge, his face set in determination as he prepared to press on through the night. His expression remained unreadable—jaw tight, brow smooth, lips pressed into a thin line. Not stoic in the heroic sense, but in the way of someone who had long since buried the luxury of reaction. His gaze lingered a moment longer on Jason's pale face before shifting to the horizon, already calculating the route forward, the weight of the hide on his back now part of his body. His survival instinct, sharpened by a lifetime of scarcity and chaos, screamed louder than fear or grief. He had no time for either.

The huskies, sensing their master's urgency, strained against the harness, eager to move, their breath steaming in the frigid air. The sledge jerked forward, cutting through the silence of the frozen landscape, the huskies' breaths misting in the cold, their pace relentless as they pulled the sledge across the ice. In the depths of the Siberian night, surrounded by silence and snow, Jason felt the boundaries between life and death dissolve. The sledge carried them onward, a fragile collection of battered bodies and weary souls, held together by the strength of one man's resolve.

***

As they crossed the lake, the stars above seemed to watch, bearing witness to this frozen odyssey, this brutal, beautiful fight for survival that bound them all together. And with each mile, Jason's mind drifted further, lulled into a state of strange tranquility, knowing that as long as the man was at the helm, they might just make it out of this wasteland alive.

The sledge cut through the snow, its runners leaving thin trails in the frost-covered earth. The world around them was suffocatingly still, save for the rhythmic whisper of the huskies' paws and the occasional crunch of snow underfoot. As they approached the village, the distant silhouette of frost-covered buildings loomed against the stark Siberian night, casting long, distorted shadows that seemed to stretch across the snow like dark fingers reaching for them.

The village was eerily quiet, most of the windows dark, as though the world itself had frozen in time. But as the sledge drew closer to the rugged, isolated hospital at the edge of the town, faint lights flickered on behind some of the glass panes. Figures watched with wide eyes, their gazes wary yet filled with a strange reverence as they recognized the man who had arrived with his pack of wolves—the man known only as **Volk**. The legends that whispered across the icy plains seemed to come to life in the form of this solitary figure, a ghost in the snow.

Volk guided the huskies to a slow stop in front of the hospital. The dogs' breath came out in short, frosty puffs, their tails flicking with anticipation. The wooden doors of the hospital swung open with a groan, and a handful of medics emerged, their footsteps muffled by the heavy snow, their expressions a blend of awe and professional focus. They moved swiftly, but their eyes lingered on Volk, recognizing him, almost in awe of the figure standing before them.

An older medic, his hair a peppered gray and his face etched with the experience of countless winters, took a cautious step forward. His gaze flickered to the bloodied bodies in the sledge, his eyes widening with a mix of respect and concern.

Old Medic (approaching cautiously, voice thick with respect in Russian):

"My pozabotimsya o nikh... Spasibo tebe"

("We'll take care of them... Thank you.")

Volk didn't reply. His face, as always, was impassive—an unreadable mask of stone. His eyes, however, carried the weight of countless years spent in the merciless cold, looking past the man in front of him and into some unseen distance. With a single nod, he stepped back, his gloved hands tightening around the reins as the medics moved with practiced haste to unload the injured.

Amelia, unconscious and pale, her face stained with dried blood, was the first to be carefully lifted from the sledge. Her body was limp, a delicate porcelain figure in the arms of the medics, the terror of her last moments frozen in the strained lines of her face.

Jason groaned weakly, clenching his side as the medics lifted him onto a stretcher, his eyes half-open but unfocused.

Khalid, barely conscious, his breathing shallow and erratic, groaned in pain as the medics adjusted him on a stretcher. His hand trembled as it gripped his side, the jagged wound on his shoulder an open testament to the tiger's deadly claws. His eyes, though clouded with exhaustion, locked briefly on Volk as he was lifted into the hospital, his lips parting in a half-hearted attempt to speak.

Inside, they rushed Khalid, Jason, and Amelia down the narrow hallway, a flurry of activity breaking out among the medical staff. Khalid, barely conscious, managed to get a phone from the medic staff, his fingers trembling as he dialed.

Khalid (hoarse, barely audible, speaking in Arabic into the phone):

"Abi... innahu Khalid. Naḥnu... naḥtāju lil-musā'ada. Kāna hunāka hujūm... namir... Amelia wa Jason..."

("Father... it's Khalid. We... we need help. There was an attack... a tiger... Amelia and Jason, they...")

His words trailed off as the weight of exhaustion overcame him. The phone slipped from his hand as his eyes fluttered closed, and the medics hurried him through the narrow hallway, a blur of white coats and sterile lights as they rushed to stabilize him and the others. The door to the treatment room slammed shut, and the faint murmur of medical voices blended with the echo of Khalid's voice, his plea for help hanging in the air.

Inside the hospital, chaos unfolded. Doctors called for gauze, sutures, antibiotics, their hands moving in practiced coordination as they worked to stem the flow of blood and stabilize the group. But the injuries were severe—more than just physical trauma. Each of them had faced death in the jaws of the tiger, and the weight of that experience would linger long after their bodies healed.

Outside, Volk stood, his posture stiff as he watched the scene unfold from the dim light of the hospital's doorway. The cold wind nipped at his face, but he didn't flinch. He had been through worse. The scent of antiseptic still clung faintly to him—he had bathed quickly, washed away the blood and grime, and now wore a clean set of borrowed clothes that hung a little loose on his frame. But even scrubbed clean, he carried the same quiet weight, the same tension in his shoulders that never fully eased. His eyes narrowed as he took in the flickering lights of the hospital, his thoughts distant, lost somewhere between the past and the present. The world around him was still, almost suffocatingly quiet, save for the low, mournful howl of the wind and the faint whisper of falling snow.

He crouched down beside his huskies, his breath fogging in the cold air as he stroked the fur of his loyal pack. Each dog met his touch with a soft, knowing whine, their eyes glowing with a strange mix of affection and reverence.

Volk (softly, feeding the huskies pieces of dried meat): *"Good dogs… strong, loyal… more loyal than most."*

A dry chuckle escaped him, a sound that held a trace of both pride and sorrow. His gloved hands patted each husky in turn, his fingers working through the fur as he gave them the comfort they had earned. The pack was his, and in their eyes, he saw more loyalty than he ever found in men. The snow continued to fall, swirling around them in a dance of cold, relentless beauty.

He stood, his eyes sweeping over the horizon, his thoughts fleeting and sharp like the snowflakes that whipped around him. The white wolf, Yuki, that always accompanied him stood by his side, its watchful eyes scanning the world with a quiet, patient wisdom. Volk's face remained unreadable as he scanned the open wilderness, where the vast, untouched expanse of snow lay waiting for him

With a final glance at the hospital, he turned and mounted the sledge once more. His movements were fluid, purposeful, as if the very act of stepping into the saddle was part of some ritual—one that had no end, only the endless journey. His grip tightened on the reins, and he paused for a moment, his silhouette a solitary figure against the swirling snow.

Without a word, he gave a sharp whistle, and the huskies surged forward, pulling the sledge into the night. The darkness closed in around him, swallowing him whole as he disappeared into the wilderness, leaving no trace behind—just the fading sound of his sled, the howl of the wind, and the quiet, relentless falling of the snow.

The last traces of his journey were erased as the snowfall covered the tracks, leaving behind only the cold, silent wilderness—a world that seemed to forget him as quickly as it had known him.

And in the hospital, the lights flickered on, but the trail of Volk and his pack had already vanished, swallowed by the vast, merciless expanse of Siberian snow.

***

The helicopters sliced through the cold Siberian air, their sleek bodies cutting through the stark white landscape. The low hum of their blades filled the quiet atmosphere, a mechanical pulse against the vast silence of the wilderness. One by one, the choppers descended toward the small airfield, their landing gear crunching through the snow with military precision. Snow swirled around as the rotors slowed, settling into a heavy stillness.

Elite medical teams hurried out of the helicopters, their movements urgent and coordinated. Clad in dark tactical gear, they carried advanced medical equipment, prepared for the worst. The air inside one of the helicopters was thick with tension.

Khalid, his face pale, lay unconscious on a stretcher. His injuries were numerous — cuts, bruises, and abrasions from the vicious attack. Beside him, the Arab king, Khalid's father, stood, his expression one of controlled panic. His mind raced, knowing that his son's life hung in the balance. The king's eyes darted between the doctors as they worked swiftly around Khalid, assessing his wounds and stabilizing him for the journey ahead.

One of the doctors, tall and composed, looked up from his work and addressed his team in a voice that was steady, yet tinged with urgency.

Doctor:

"They're stable for now, but we need to get them to a proper facility fast. They won't make it otherwise."

Khalid's father, unable to keep the worry from his face, watched the doctor closely, then immediately turned his attention to his phone. His fingers, trembling with anxiety, dialed a number. His voice, though strained, was filled with a calm authority.

Arab King (into the phone, in Arabic):

"Ta'akkad min anna afḍal al-akhisā'iyyīn fī intizārinā fī al-mustashfā. Ḥayāt ibnī laysat mawḍi' tafāwuḍ."

("Make sure the best specialists are waiting at the hospital. My son's life is not up for negotiation.")

He ended the call, the weight of his words hanging in the air. As the helicopter lifted off, Khalid, still drifting in and out of consciousness, glanced out of the window. His gaze swept over the vast, endless expanse of snow-covered wilderness below. The beauty of it was undeniable — vast stretches of white, broken only by the occasional cluster of trees or a distant, jagged peak rising in the distance. For a moment, he felt an odd connection to the land, as if it had somehow become a part of him now.

But that fleeting moment of peace was interrupted by a movement — a dark shape cutting through the snow, solitary and deliberate against the vast white. Khalid's heart skipped a beat as his eyes focused on the distant figure: a man pulling a sledge, barely more than a silhouette against the frozen horizon. There was something almost ethereal about the scene — the quiet determination in the man's stride, the stillness of the world around him. It was haunting and awe-inspiring all at once, as if the wilderness itself had chosen him to walk its path.

Khalid's breath caught in his chest.

Khalid (whispering to himself, his voice barely audible):

"Who... was that man?"

The figure of Volk stood like a shadow against the brilliance of the snow, a solitary figure whose presence seemed to pulse with power. Khalid's eyes narrowed, trying to make sense of what he saw — not just the figure in the snow now, but the entire sequence of events that had led to this moment. The tiger. The chaos. The man who had appeared like a phantom and saved them. His mind, clouded by exhaustion and shock, scrambled to recall the details — a face, a voice, a name — but everything felt fragmented, like pieces of a dream slipping away the harder he tried to hold on. The man remained indistinct, more myth than memory, hovering at the edge of Khalid's fading consciousness.

Inside the helicopter, Amelia's father paced anxiously, his face drawn with worry. His phone was pressed to his ear, his voice tight as he coordinated the evacuation.

Amelia's Father (into the phone, voice laced with urgency):

"We need a full medical team at the hospital, and make sure they're prepared for multiple trauma cases. Call whoever you need to call."

The helicopter continued to climb, the wild, unrelenting beauty of the Siberian terrain stretching out below. But Khalid's mind was elsewhere, still haunted by the vision of the man in the snow. Who was he? How had he arrived at the scene? And why had he come to their aid? The mystery of it gnawed at him, leaving him with a thousand unanswered questions.

As the helicopter ascended higher, the Arab king leaned closer to his son. His voice was soft, but there was an unmistakable sense of resolve in it.

Arab King (gently, but with determination):

"Satakūnu bikhayr, yā bunayya. A'iduka annanā sanatajāwaz hādhā ma'an."

("You're going to be okay, my son. I promise you; we'll get through this together.")

Khalid nodded weakly, his body still aching from the ordeal. But the words, though comforting, couldn't ease the tension in his mind. His thoughts returned to the figure in the snow. The man who had intervened when they needed help most. The man who, despite everything, remained a mystery.

Amelia's father, his face a mixture of concern and respect, watched Khalid quietly for a moment before speaking again, his voice softer now.

Amelia's Father (sighing, almost to himself):

"I never wanted this for you guys, Khalid. But you have proven your strength today. Thank you, son."

Khalid's gaze shifted to him, a faint, appreciative nod, the only response he could muster. The helicopter hummed through the sky, its engines working in harmony with the relentless winds outside. But Khalid's mind remained fixed on one thought, one image: the figure in the snow, standing alone, a dark shadow against the whiteness. Who was he?

The helicopter soared higher, leaving the cold Siberian landscape behind. The pain in Khalid's body was nothing compared to the weight of the mystery that lingered in his mind. Would he ever find the answers he sought about the man who had saved them all?

The Messiah

The cafe was a sanctuary from the cold evening outside, its warmth offering a soft reprieve compared to the biting Siberian air. The dim lighting wrapped the room in a comforting glow, and the subtle aroma of coffee and burning wax from the candles on the altar filled the space. Against the far wall, photographs of Elly—her vibrant smile captured in each frame—lined the space, a quiet tribute to the girl they had all lost. The flickering candlelight cast shadows on the images, making them seem almost alive. Each picture showed her in a moment of joy, the essence of who she was still lingering in the air.

A handful of people moved around the room in hushed reverence, sharing memories of Elly, the murmurs of their conversations blending into the peaceful ambiance. But at the back of the room, three figures stood apart from the rest. They were united by the traumatic bond sthey shared but separated by the silence of the past year.

Khalid stood by the altar, his eyes fixed on Elly's photograph, his posture heavy with the weight of regret. His hands were loosely folded in front of him, but he barely seemed to notice them. His expression was distant, as if the passage of time had done little to dull the ache in his chest.

Jason leaned back against a nearby table; his expression was unreadable. The faint scars on his face seemed insignificant compared to the deeper, invisible ones that marked him. His eyes were shadowed, and though he remained still, there was a sense of constant tension about him.

Amelia sat beside him, her arms tightly crossed as if to shield herself from the vulnerability of the moment. She glanced at Khalid from time to time, her gaze flickering with concern and uncertainty.

The silence between them was thick, the kind of silence only a year of grief could create. It was an unspoken understanding, the weight of loss between them was too heavy to break easily.

Jason's voice cut through the stillness, breaking the silence with a smirk that didn't quite reach his eyes. He spoke with the dark humor of someone trying to mask the pain beneath.

"So... didn't think we'd ever be here again. Thought the tiger took us out for good."

Amelia wrapped her arms tighter around herself, the cold of the night creeping back into her bones despite the warmth of the room. Her voice was soft, almost a whisper, but her words carried the weight of the past year.

"Feels like we're back there, doesn't it? Like it never left us."

Khalid's gaze shifted toward Elly's photo. His voice was quieter now, the guilt in it palpable as he spoke. The words seemed to weigh him down, heavy with regret and a sense of helplessness.

"It did more than leave marks on us, Amelia. It took Elly."

His eyes lingered on her photo for a long moment before they flicked back to the others.

"I should've been stronger for all of us..."

Jason's interruption was firm, a shift in tone that commanded attention. He stepped closer to Khalid, his words carrying the quiet authority of someone who had faced their own demons.

"You were. We all fought. But that man saved us... whoever he was."

Amelia's eyes softened as she nodded slowly, her mind drifting back to the memory of the lone figure in the snow. It was a haunting image, one that had stayed with her, even in the quiet moments when they thought they could finally move on.

"I still think about him," She said quietly, her voice distant.

"He showed up out of nowhere... like some spirit."

The words hung in the air, the three of them lost in the memory of that night—the cold, the terror, and the strange, silent figure who had come to their rescue. There was no explanation, no rational understanding of what had happened. Just a quiet mystery that lingered in their minds.

Khalid broke the silence, his voice heavy with something between frustration and curiosity. He was still searching for answers, even after everything that had passed.

"I tried to trace him when I recovered. Pulled every security contact I had. But the truth is... he's a ghost."

Khalid exhaled slowly, his eyes flickering briefly to the photo of Elly once more.

"No one knows who he really is, where he came from. Among the locals, he's a messiah, some kind of legend."

Jason and Amelia exchanged a glance, the unease in their eyes unmistakable. The figure who had saved them—the man who had appeared out of nowhere and disappeared just as quickly—was still an enigma. A mystery that none of them could solve. It was as if he had never truly been there at all, just a fleeting shadow in their lives. But the memory of him lingered, unresolved.

The cafe was quiet again, the flickering candlelight casting long shadows on the wall. The weight of the past year pressed down on them, but even in the silence, there was a strange sense of connection—an unspoken bond that had formed between them. A bond that would never be broken, no matter how much time had passed.

***

The hospital was silent except for the muffled voices of nurses in the hallway and the hum of medical equipment. The walls seemed to absorb the sound, leaving only the faintest echoes of life. Inside, two large Arab bodyguards, their faces unreadable, leaned in closer, their attention fully on the Old Medic as he spoke. His voice was low and steady, yet it carried a weight that demanded attention.

"Volk... that's what people call him,", The Old Medic began, his eyes darkening as if haunted by memories.

"But he is no ordinary man."

He paused, his gaze flickering between the two bodyguards, as though testing their patience before continuing.

"There's an old story here, one that's been passed down for generations. It dates back some 600 years."

He let the words hang in the air for a moment, as though bracing for their disbelief. Then, without waiting for a response, he pressed on.

"One of our ancestors was crossing the Siberian plains when an earthquake struck. The land shook violently, and an avalanche swept down from the mountains. He survived, barely. But when the snow settled, something strange was uncovered. A cavern in the glacier—hidden for centuries—opened up. Inside, there was a red, radiant stone. It was mesmerizing, unlike anything from this world."

The Old Medic's voice dropped even lower as he continued. The room seemed to grow colder, his words carrying the weight of a forgotten curse.

"When the ancestor brought that stone back to his village, everything changed. What he didn't know was that the stone had trapped something—something ancient, something dangerous. Creatures bound by the stone's magic for centuries. We call them the Valkaris."

The first bodyguard frowned, clearly skeptical.

"Valkaris?"

The Old Medic nodded grimly.

"They are undead, remnants of an ancient curse. If you so much as lay eyes on them, they know. Even hidden, they can sense you. And once they find you, they bite. If you're bitten, you become one of them—a mindless predator."

The second bodyguard scoffed; his disbelief was evident.

"Like some... plague?"

The Old Medic leaned in, his gaze intense, locking eyes with the two men.

"Over time, our ancestors adapted. The village was built high on a cliff, the only safe place in this desolate land. Nothing grows here, but there is gold—plenty of it. And that's what brought miners, mercenaries, the brave and the desperate. They came to scale the cliffs, to descend into the frozen lakes in search of riches. But many never returned. Not all of them were prepared for the Valkaris."

***

The landscape was harsh, unforgiving. The winds whipped through the air, biting and relentless, as the village clung to the edge of a towering cliff. The outpost sat at the precipice, a gathering of people hardened by the elements and their dangerous work. The vast stretch of Siberian plains rolled out before them, an endless white sea, but here at the cliff's edge, life still flickered in the form of miners and mercenaries who made their living by extracting gold from the land.

Among the crowd were two towering Russian brothers, their faces scarred by the cold, their eyes as hard as the frozen earth beneath their boots. The twins were as much a part of the landscape as the cliffs they worked on. Their heavy steps echoed on the ground as they surveyed the scene, their expressions unreadable.

An agent, small and wiry, approached them, leading a figure who was the complete opposite of everything in this village. Volk. He moved with a predator's grace, his lean frame standing in stark contrast to the bulk of the twins. His gaze was flat, emotionless, but there was something in his eyes—something chilling. A cigar dangled loosely from his lips, the faintest trail of smoke rising into the cold air.

The agent spoke in a smooth, oily tone, the words almost slipping from his mouth as he introduced the newcomer.

"This is our man. Fearless as they come."

The twins didn't say a word, merely exchanging a brief glance before nodding in unison. The agent took the silence as approval and gestured for Volk to follow. After a moment of hushed exchanges between the brothers and the agent, one of the twins handed over a worn leather bag. It clinked with the unmistakable sound of gold. The agent pocketed the bag with a wide grin, turning back to Volk.

"Take care out there."

He said, his voice dripping with an unspoken expectation of some reaction. But Volk remained unmoved, his blank expression unchanging.

Without a word, Volk turned and followed the twins into the heart of the outpost, his figure merging with theirs as they moved through the crowd. There was no grand greeting, no celebration—just a man walking silently, as if nothing in this world could stir him.

***

The room was dim, lit only by the pale slivers of moonlight that filtered through a narrow, barred window. The shadows in the corners seemed to stretch and twitch with the quiet stillness that enveloped the space. The floor, covered with a thick, weathered sheepskin carpet, felt cold despite the lack of wind. The room itself felt like a prison—a place where time stood still, as if it had been forgotten.

Volk stirred in the darkness, his body moving with quiet precision, the only sound the soft scrape of his boots on the floor. He moved toward the door, opened it, and stepped out into the stillness of the night. The twin brothers waited just outside, their forms looming in the dim light.

A brief exchange of nods passed between them, and without another word, they led Volk down the hall and into the next chamber.

The hall was alive with noise. Laughter echoed off the stone walls, and the clinking of glasses mixed with the boisterous chatter of those gathered around the long wooden table. The air was thick with the scent of hearty food and alcohol. The people at the table—rough-edged, intimidating—paused in their revelry as Volk entered, his presence commanding attention. The room seemed to hold its breath for a moment as his gaze swept over the crowd. A sense of unease rippled through the room, though no one dared voice it.

The first twin, his chest puffed out with pride, raised his glass in a grand gesture.

"Ladies and gentlemen, welcome our new member—Volk!"

The room erupted into applause and cheers; glasses raised in a raucous toast. The warmth of the welcome was palpable, though it didn't quite reach Volk. He nodded in acknowledgment, his expression unchanged, and scanned the room. Every pair of eyes in the hall was on him, some filled with curiosity, others with caution. The air hummed with anticipation.

The first twin continued, his voice booming through the hall.

"We've heard stories of him from the Arab world. Word has it, he and his mentor completed an impossible mission—only the two of them survived. Now that his mentor's out of the game, Volk's found his way here. Let's see how true the myths about him really are."

The gang erupted in cheers once more, raising their glasses in another toast to Volk. He stood still, his focus unbroken, scanning the room with an air of quiet contemplation. The walls were lined with weapons—

rifles, knives, tools of war—and the air itself seemed thick with violence. But Volk was unmoved, as if he belonged here more than anyone.

Volk's gaze settled on a table cluttered with knives and pistols. Moving with calm confidence, he approached and picked up one of the blades. He examined it closely, as if contemplating its purpose, before his attention shifted to an old clock mounted on the far wall. For a moment, he stood there, as if waiting for the perfect moment. The hall buzzed with noise; the atmosphere charged with anticipation. As the clock struck 8:59 PM, Volk's arm moved with lightning speed. Without hesitation, the knife flew from his hand in one fluid motion, embedding itself in the clock face with a sharp thud, just grazing the second hand as it ticked past the five-second mark. The room fell into stunned silence, the cheers dying out as all eyes turned to him.

Without waiting, Volk threw another knife, this time hitting the 10-second mark with deadly accuracy but missing the second hand again by a thread. Then another, hitting the 15-second mark. The knives continued to fly, each one marking the time with perfect precision but missing the hand by a thread. As the tension in the room grew, a collective gasp filled the air when Volk shattered the hour hand with a final throw at the 45-second mark.

The silence was deafening. Volk stood, still and composed, as the room watched in awe, he continued. Finally, he picked up two knives and, without blinking, threw them simultaneously at 09:00 pm. One knife struck the second and minute hands, and the other pierced the center of the clock with a sharp metallic clank, dislodging the machinery. The room erupted into deafening applause, the rhythmic beat of clinking whiskey glasses reverberating in the air as the crowd chanted his name:

"Volk! Volk! Volk!"

The first twin strode over to him, pulling him into a tight, brotherly embrace, his grin wide and triumphant.

"Welcome to the team."

***

The map was spread across the table, its edges curling slightly under the weight of various relics, scattered notes, and assorted equipment. A fire crackled in the hearth, its orange glow casting long, flickering shadows across the cold stone walls, creating an eerie dance of light and dark in the room. The group stood around the table, their faces bathed in the soft firelight, each one focused on the task ahead. The air was thick with tension, yet there was an unspoken understanding between them — they were all in this together, no matter the cost.

The First Twin leaned forward, his brow furrowed in concentration as he traced a route with his finger, his movements slow and deliberate.

"This is where we'll go,"

He said, his voice was steady but laced with an edge of forewarning. He paused, looking each of them in the eye.

"But remember—those who've taken this path before... never came back."

Volk met his gaze with unwavering calm. The warning, though grim, did not faze him. His eyes moved over the map with a practiced focus, memorizing every contour of the treacherous terrain. There was no room for doubt. Only preparation.

The Second Twin's voice was low, filled with a weight that matched the dark look on his face. He leaned in, his gaze hardening as he added,

"We must be careful. Avoid all blood. If anyone's injured... we leave them behind and hide until morning. Anyone who dies, dies. We close our eyes, cover ourselves, and wait for the terror to pass."

He paused; his eyes locked with each of theirs.

"And above all—silence. Even the smallest sound, even your breath, could betray you."

The weight of his words hung heavily in the room, casting a shadow that no firelight could banish. The First Twin reached into his cloak, pulling out a small, worn leather pouch. He opened it carefully and extracted a Red Stone, placing it in front of Volk with deliberate slowness. The stone gleamed faintly in the dim light, its surface alive with an eerie glow.

"When we find the cave, this is where it must stay,"

The First Twin said, his tone now colder, more serious.

"And if we make it out alive,"

he continued, the gravity of his words settling heavily upon them,

"we seal that cave. For good. No one can know what we find there."

Volk's gaze never left the Red Stone. His eyes were fixed on it, his expression unreadable, but his mind was already working, calculating, weighing the enormity of the task ahead. There was no hesitation, no second thoughts — only resolve. He understood the stakes. He knew the risks. And he was ready.

***

The wilderness of Siberia stretched out before them, harsh and unforgiving. The team moved through the snow, navigating the icy landscape with cautious precision. Half of the group had made it to the bottom of a steep glacier, while the others carefully descended behind them. A freezing river rushed alongside; its power evident in the roar of the current.

"The water's freezing, and the current's strong.", the First Twin warned.

"Stay alert."

The group pressed on, the land around them a brutal test of survival. They reached a frozen lake, its surface solid but treacherous, a deceptive calm masking the danger beneath. The team continued, knowing the threats the wilderness hid, their every movement measured.

Suddenly, an accident. A gear malfunction caused one of the women to slip down the rope, crashing into another team member below her. A drop of blood trickled from her nose, splattering across the First Twin's coat. But no one noticed it or paused to check on her. They moved forward; their goal was clear.

Night fell, and the chilling howls of wolves echoed through the darkness, sending a shiver through the group. They kept moving, relentless in their pursuit.

Then came the rumble. A sound that shook the air, sending fear into their hearts. A herd of Valkaris appeared, charging toward them with terrifying speed. The creatures were monstrous, their bluish skin, wolverine-like teeth, and claws like a tiger's. Panic spreads like wildfire. The team scattered, but it was too late.

The First Twin was the first to be attacked. The others fell into the icy waters, the brutal current sweeping them away. One by one, they were taken, their fates sealed beneath the ice.

Volk, Alexi, and Nadia were the only ones left.

Nadia was the first to be struck. A Valkari lunged, its teeth sinking into her neck. She slipped onto the ice, carried away by the current, her body dragged beneath the water along with the creature. Alexi fought back desperately, blocking another Valkari's jaws with his climbing gear. The struggle sent him sliding toward the river, the beast still attached to him.

Volk turned just in time to avoid another Valkari's lunge, sidestepping as it crashed into a jagged glacier. He finished the creature off swiftly, then bolted, his heart pounding in his chest. The ice beneath him cracked with a sudden, terrifying jolt. Volk plunged through the frozen surface, the freezing water swallowing him whole. His body screamed in shock, the cold so intense it felt as though it could freeze his very soul. Blood mingled with the water as he fought to keep himself afloat, the freezing depths draining his strength with each passing second.

The current was relentless, pulling him further under. He struggled to stay conscious, his heart pounding in his chest, every movement a battle against the freezing grip of the water. His body, numb and aching, finally managed to find purchase on the broken ice, his hands scraping against the jagged edges as he pulled himself forward.

With desperate strength, he pushed himself onto a larger chunk of ice that had broken off, now drifting with the current toward the far side of the lake. The Valkaris, stranded on the other side, were unable to cross the fractured ice. Volk's teeth chattered as he floated, gasping for breath, trying to make sense of his surroundings.

Eventually, the current carried him to the edge of the lake, where the ice had broken enough for him to scramble onto solid ground. He gasped in the frigid air, his body aching as he stumbled forward, his legs shaky beneath him.

The harsh wilderness was still around him, cold and unforgiving. He ran, heart pounding, desperate for shelter. He spotted a cluster of bushes nearby, their thick branches offering some cover. His breath came in ragged gasps as he dove behind them, seeking refuge from the terror of the night.

It was there, amidst the chaos and the bloodshed, that Volk found them. Two wolf puppies, shivering with fear, huddled beside their mother, her eyes wild with the instinct to protect. The mother growled softly, a low rumble of warning as Volk knelt beside them, his breath fogging in the cold air. He moved with caution, understanding the fragility of the moment. His hands were steady as he kept the puppies quiet, his fingers brushing over their soft fur, urging them to remain silent.

The night wore on, the terror of the battle still fresh in Volk's mind. The darkness was cold, heavy and suffocating, but it was nothing compared to the silence that followed.

As the first light of dawn broke over the Siberian mountains, the sun's rays cast a pale, golden light over the icy terrain. The nightmare of the night seemed distant, though the sound of wild dogs scurrying through the underbrush reminded Volk that danger was never far behind. He emerged from the bushes, cautious, his breath visible in the crisp morning air, but the terror of the night still echoed in his bones.

He had survived. But what had they lost? And what waited ahead?

He glanced around, eyes scanning the rugged landscape.

"Is it over?", he thought, uncertainty weighing heavily on his mind. He began to move upward, careful with each step as he searched for any sign of his former team. After what felt like hours, he stumbled upon their abandoned luggage, a relic of the chaos that had unfolded the previous night. Alone now, he gathered what little supplies he could find and he found the red stone, clinging to the remnants of his past.

"I must keep going," he reminded himself, his voice quiet in his mind.

Days blurred into weeks as he traversed the desolate wilderness, becoming fully self-sufficient. The harsh, unforgiving environment had shaped him into something different, stronger, more resilient. For two long years, Volk lived as part of the wild. Whatever elite training he once had—military, tactical, disciplined—meant nothing out here. The wilderness had no use for commands or codes. It demanded instinct, silence, and savagery. He hunted with the wolves, slept beneath the stars, and learned the ways of the land through the language of blood and survival.

He didn't just adapt—he transformed. No longer a man trained by human systems, he became something else entirely: a creature of the cold, a shadow among predators. His mind sharpened, not through strategy, but through silence. His body moved with the rhythm of the wilderness, not drills. He had become a wild animal that knew how to kill like animals do—quiet, fast, without remorse.

After two years of isolation, disconnected from the world, Volk finally discovered the cave nestled within the mountains. It was the sanctuary he had been searching for. His clothes were tattered, replaced by a rugged bear pelt draped over his shoulders. His body was chiseled, the muscles honed from relentless training and hunting. Volk had become a formidable figure, the alpha of a wild pack of wolves that now followed him. Among them were the two wolf pups that were now adults, one white, one black, who had become his companions.

Volk knelt in front of the cave, his heart heavy with the weight of everything he had been through. He had finally found it.

He carefully placed the red stone at the spot mentioned by the brothers, performing the ritual they had described. Memories flooded back, and he bowed his head in respect, honoring the twins who had fallen during their journey. With a makeshift stone hammer he had crafted from the wilderness, he began to break through the glaciers to close the cave, a symbolic act of rebirth and strength.

And as the ice shattered around him, Volk stood amidst the chaos of falling snow and ice, embodying a presence that was almost otherworldly, a messiah ready to face whatever came next.

***

The old medic, now spoke of Volk's journey to those who had gathered. The bodyguards stood nearby, their eyes wide in disbelief as they absorbed this tale of survival and transformation. Old Medic,

"And so, he became the people's messiah..."

The King's Resolve

The quiet hum of the cafe enveloped Khalid, Amelia, and Jason as they sat at a dimly lit booth, the weight of the story lingering between them. The candle on the table flickered, casting dancing shadows across their faces, intensifying the somber mood. Khalid's gaze was distant, his thoughts lost in the haunting memories of the man who had saved them. His memories were scattered, almost mythical, as if the man existence was unbelievable.

In the back corner of the cafe, dressed in a tailored suit, the Arab King sat, leaning slightly forward, absorbed in their conversation. He sipped from his cup slowly, contemplatively, his face a mask of disbelief and awe. His eyes were fixed on them, as if trying to hold on to each word, each detail.

Inside him, a resolve began to take shape.

"I must find this man... and repay my debt.", he thought, the weight of his duty pressing down on him.

He cleared his throat, breaking the thick silence that had fallen over the table. Amelia looked up, her expression softening, the memories flooding back. Though much of the time had blurred, there was a deep reverence for the mysterious figure who had stepped into their lives like a shadow and disappeared just as quickly.

"It's strange," she said, her voice tinged with awe.

"I can't even remember his face. It's like... a blur, a shadow."

Khalid turned to her, his expression grave yet respectful.

"That's who he is. A ghost. He survives like no other. He roams those Siberian plains with wolves by his side, vanishing into thin air. His whereabouts? Impossible to know."

The King's eyes grew sharper, his curiosity evident, but there was something deeper in his gaze—a sense of duty.

"Khalid, my son,"

He came closer, his voice low yet commanding,

"Why have you never told me about this man? Our kingdom owes him an unpayable debt. As sheikhs, we do not accept help without giving something in return."

His words settled over the table like a heavy mantle.

"We will find him. I will send my best men, my finest scouts, to track him down."

Jason, who had been silent up to this point, looked up with a mixture of skepticism and something else—something like reverence for the mysterious savior.

"How could anyone find him?", he asked, his voice tinged with doubt.

"He vanishes like the snow in the wind."

Amelia nodded, leaning into the table, her eyes wide.

"But we have to try, don't we? There's so much more we don't know about him... I still wonder who he is and where he came from."

The Arab King leaned back in a chair, his presence commanding the room even in the silence. His fingers drummed lightly against the polished wood of the table, as if weighing the gravity of what had been said. His gaze, however, had already hardened with resolve.

"Consider it taken care of," he said.

"Tell me, what more do you remember of him? Any detail could help. I will search every corner of this earth to uncover this man."

Khalid hesitated for a moment, his mind racing back to the frozen terrain, to the figure in the snow, the way the cold air had stung his lungs, the crunch of snow underfoot. He spoke slowly, as if pulling the memory from deep within.

"I... I think I could help a sketch artist piece together his face. I remember his eyes. They held... something beyond human. And there was... a tattoo on his arm. Familiar, like a symbol I've seen before, but I can't remember where."

Amelia nodded, a memory sparking in her own mind.

"Yes, his eyes... they were unlike any I'd ever seen. And that tattoo... it was something ancient, something almost mythical."

A tense silence filled the space between them, their reverence for the man who had saved their lives growing deeper, heavier with each passing second. Finally, the Arab King took out his gold-plated phone, its surface gleaming under the dim cafe lights. He dialed with purpose, his voice carrying an edge of command.

"Aḥmad, jahhiz afḍal rassām burturih li-yakūn fī al-funduq 'inda 'awdatinā."

("Ahmed, arrange for the best portrait artist to be at the hotel when we return.")

"Bil-ṭab' Ayuha al-malik"

("Of course, my King.")

Ahmed, the king's loyal companion, responded on phone.

The King lowered the phone and turned to the group.

"Let's make our way back to the suite."

They rose from the booth, the weight of their mission grounding their movements, each step a march toward the unknown. Outside, a sleek, gold-plated Rolls Royce awaited them. The polished exterior gleamed under the city lights. The driver opened the door, and one by one, they climbed inside, the luxurious leather seats sinking beneath them as they settled in.

As the car glided through the streets, moving past the Waldorf Astoria, Amelia stared out the window. Her thoughts drifted back to that figure in the snow, surrounded by wolves, a shadow among shadows. She couldn't shake the mystery of who he was, of the tattoo, of the fragments of memory that seemed both distant and present.

Jason clenched his hands, a strange mix of admiration and unease coursing through him. He couldn't help but wonder about the man who had been there when they needed him most.

Khalid sat silently, a faint smile playing on his lips, his eyes gleaming with something that might have been hope, or perhaps closure.

The caravan of sleek black SUVs moved through the city streets, engines humming in unison, cutting through traffic with precision. The wail of police sirens cleared the path, their urgency marking the seriousness of the occasion. As they approached the Blair House, diplomats and dignitaries stood at the entrance, waiting to greet the Arab King. He steps out, nodding briefly to acknowledge them but moving with a purposeful stride, an urgency that commands silence from those around him. Sensing the gravity of the moment, the gathering of officials and diplomats watch as he and his companions make their way inside.

Inside the grand lobby of the president's guest house, the air was thick with anticipation. The King and his companions walked across the polished marble floor, their footsteps echoing in the vastness of the room. The property manager hurried to meet them, flanked by three sketch artists, each carrying drawing sheets, tablets, and laptops, ready to begin their task.

The King and his party move toward the elevator, followed by the sketch artists and the manager. An elevator operator quickly joins them, and the elevator doors close with a quiet chime, leaving the remaining entourage and sketch artists to take the next elevator.

In the suite, the atmosphere was heavy with the importance of the task at hand. The King and his companions settled on plush couches; their faces marked by the tension of the moment. Ahmed—a muscular, broad-shouldered man, the King's loyal companion, stood by the door, his eyes scanning the room with a practiced vigilance. The three sketch artists entered, their movements swift and purposeful. Without a word, they set up their equipment, the silence between them thickening as they prepared to bring the ghostly figure from the past into form.

The King sat forward; his eyes sharp as he addressed the artists.

"Gentlemen," he said, his voice unwavering,

"I want you to sketch a man's portrait as lifelike as possible. This is an urgent matter."

The artists nodded, the seriousness of the task clear in their focused expressions. They began to work, their hands moving swiftly over drawing sheets, tablets, and laptops.

Khalid and Amelia sat close by, speaking in low murmurs as they recalled fragments of the past, their words blending into the quiet of the room. Jason watched, his gaze fixed on the artists as they worked, his mind spinning with thoughts of the man whose face was now taking shape before them.

One artist worked intently on a digital version of the face, adding intricate details, while another focused on recreating the tattoo, based on Khalid's and Amelia's descriptions.

The whir of the printer filled the air as the final sketch took form, the edges crisp and sharp, as if the past had come back to life in that single image.

The head artist approached the King, presenting the finished portrait with a slight bow.

"Your Highness."

The King took the sketch into his hands, his eyes scanning the face before him.

Recognition flickered in his gaze—something more than mere familiarity, but a deep sense of reverence. The face was rugged, powerful, and the eyes held something that went beyond human.

Another artist stepped forward, presenting an image of the tattoo.

The King's voice was steady, filled with resolve.

"Send this tattoo image to every tattoo artist and every tattoo festival across the world. Offer a reward to anyone who recognizes this man or can tell us who made this tattoo."

He turned to Ahmed, pressing the image of the tattoo into his hands.

"Also, send our best scouts to Siberia. Tell them to search every corner. I want to know this man's location, every detail. When they find him, we'll go meet him ourselves."

Ahmed nodded, his fingers already moving quickly over his phone as he began carrying out the King's orders. The King remained still, his eyes fixed on the portrait, lost in thought. His resolve was clear—this was just the beginning of a much greater journey, one that would uncover a man shrouded in mystery and legend.

The image of the portrait lingered in the air, the man's face imprinted on the King's mind, his resolve growing stronger with every passing moment.

Dead Ends and the Listening King

The rugged landscape of Ladakh stretched endlessly before them, the golden sands of the desert mountains rising sharply against the brilliant blue sky. The black Mercedes SUV, sleek and imposing, weaved its way along the winding mountain road, its tires gripping the smooth asphalt with precision. Two more black SUVs flanked the vehicle, accompanied by a pair of army jeeps. The convoy moved with an air of formidable protection, cutting through this remote terrain as if it belonged to them.

Inside the SUV, the atmosphere was one of quiet anticipation, though fatigue hung heavy in the air. Amelia, curled in the seat beside Khalid, slowly stirred from her nap. Her eyes blinked against the sunlight streaming through the tinted windows, casting a soft glow across her face. She stretched her arms above her head, the motion revealing the weariness of the long journey.

"How much longer do we have?", she asked, her voice was still thick with sleep.

Khalid glanced at the GPS mounted on the dashboard, his fingers brushing over the screen as he checked their location.

"About 20 minutes. But look at this view," he added, his voice filled with awe

He gestured toward the window, and Amelia turned her head. The vast, untamed landscape unfolded before them. In the distance, a monastery perched high on a cliffside, its stone walls glowing in the fading light of the afternoon. Monks in bright robes stood outside, their chants rising and falling in the air like a melody, bringing a sense of peace to the otherwise harsh surroundings.

The convoy continued its steady pace, moving deeper into the mountainous region. The breathtaking beauty of the land passed by in a blur, the colors of the earth shifting with every turn of the road.

Then, the stillness of the moment was broken by the sharp ring of Khalid's phone. He reached for it instinctively, answering the call without hesitation.

"Abie?"

("Father?")

The King:

"Khalid, laqad wajadnā ar-rajul. ʿUd wa daʿnā nadhhab li-muqābaltih.

("Khalid, we've found the man. Come back, and let's go meet him.")

Khalid (looking at Amelia, who senses the shift):

"Naḥnu ʿalā washk al-wuṣūl ilā qaryat hādhā al-fannān. Daʿīnā nataḥaqqaq minhu marra ʾakhīra."

("We're almost at the village of this artist. Let's check him out one last time.")

The King (firmly):

"Idhā lam tatatābaq al-qiṣṣa, fa-lā tuḍiʿ al-mazeed min al-waqt. Daʿnā nasmaʿ min ar-rajul nafsih."

("If the story doesn't match, don't waste more time. Let's hear from the man himself.")

Khalid (with resolve):

"Bil-ta'kīd yā abī, sanaʿūd ghadan."

("Of course, Father. We'll be back tomorrow.")

The King:

"Saʾaṭlub min Basheer an yurattib riḥlatanā. Arāk ḥīnaha."

("I'll ask Basheer to arrange our trip. I'll see you then.")

Khalid disconnected the call and turned toward Amelia, a look of quiet determination etched on his face.

"Our men have tracked him down. We're going to meet him."

Amelia's exhaustion seemed to lift in an instant, replaced by a wave of excitement. A smile broke across her face, her eyes lighting up with the anticipation of what lay ahead. '

"Finally! I can't wait to meet him."

The SUV slowed as they neared the village. Khalid glanced out the window, taking in the scenery with a sense of appreciation for the rugged beauty of the place. The village was small, nestled in the shadows of towering peaks, a peaceful oasis in the harsh landscape of Ladakh.

The convoy pulled to a gentle stop at the edge of the village. Khalid looked at the landscape one last time, his eyes scanning the horizon.

"Let's hope this man is worth the journey,"

He said, his tone was a mixture of curiosity and skepticism.

Amelia, her excitement palpable, nodded eagerly.

"Let's see if he holds the key to everything we've been searching for."

As the vehicle came to a halt, the doors opened, and the team began to step out, their boots crunching against the gravel road. They were close now—so close to the artist who could hold the answers they had been seeking. The journey, the long hours of uncertainty, had led them to this moment. And they were ready.

The village of Turtuk stretched before them like something out of a dream. Quaint and serene, it exuded an almost untouched beauty, with the daily rhythm of village life unfolding in every corner. Women in colorful shawls tended to their homes, children played in the dirt roads, and the smell of freshly baked bread wafted from nearby ovens. It was peaceful—a stark contrast to the harsh, rugged terrain surrounding it.

Khalid's gaze swept over the village with a look of perplexity. This wasn't the kind of place one would expect to find a man like Volk, whose very presence seemed to belong to a different world—gritty, hardened, and enigmatic. But this village was the complete opposite. It was tranquil, as if untouched by the chaos of the outside world.

He turned to Amelia and Ahmed, both of whom stood beside him, observing the village with cautious eyes. His voice was skeptical, cutting through the stillness as he muttered,

"I hope this isn't another wild claim. Look at these people—there's no way anyone here resembles Volk."

His words hung in the air as they all stepped out of the Mercedes SUV. The sound of the car doors slamming shut seemed out of place in this peaceful setting, breaking the calm as a group of Z-security personnel emerged around them. Dressed in black suits and dark sunglasses, the imposing figures moved with military precision, their vigilance palpable. They formed a protective circle around Khalid and his team, their eyes scanning the surroundings, ever watchful.

The villagers, who had never seen such a display of authority, watched with a mix of awe and confusion. A few curious faces peeked from behind rooftops or around corners, eyes wide with wonder. It wasn't every day that the quiet village of Turtuk played host to such an entourage. The air was thick with curiosity and uncertainty, the foreign presence disrupting the otherwise harmonious rhythm of the village.

As the royal group moved deeper into the village, the silence was broken by the approach of a local man. He was weathered but friendly, his brown eyes steady with respect. He bowed slightly, acknowledging their presence before speaking in a soft but clear voice.

"I'm Sonam," he said, his tone both formal and welcoming.

"I've been asked to guide you."

Khalid studied him for a moment, his skepticism still evident, but he didn't question the man's introduction. Sonam was their guide, and there was no time for hesitation now. He nodded curtly, his eyes scanning the surroundings one last time.

"Lead the way," Khalid said, his voice low but firm.

Sonam gave a slight bow and turned, leading them deeper into the village. As they moved, the villagers slowly began to return to their daily lives, though their eyes often lingered on the strangers, their curiosity unabated. It was a place where nothing much changed, and yet, today, something felt different—something big was about to unfold.

The group arrived at Tashi's home; a modest dwelling nestled on the edge of the valley. The house itself was simple, with a small lawn that sloped gently down toward the stunning view of the valley below. The landscape stretched out like a painting—rolling hills, distant snow-capped peaks, and the gentle hum of nature all around. Despite the beauty of the surroundings, the small yard felt almost too humble for the guests who had just arrived.

Plastic chairs, cheap and weathered from years of use, were scattered haphazardly across the lawn. The setup was a far cry from the regal environment that Khalid and his entourage were accustomed to. Inside, the sound of clinking dishes and the faint aroma of tea being prepared drifted from the small kitchen where Tashi's wife, Dolma, worked diligently.

Sonam, who had been leading the way, stopped short as he surveyed the scene. His expression shifted from the calm demeanor of a local guide to one of clear irritation. He pulled Tashi aside, his voice low but sharp.

"Handang! Enna tsoks kursi rig mane mathoba

("Are you foolish? Couldn't you come up with better chairs than these?")

Sonam whispered, his frustration palpable.

Tashi, ever the easygoing man, grinned at the comment, shrugging nonchalantly.

""Chi dug e kursi na?

("What's wrong with these chairs?")

He asked, his tone light and playful.

Sonam's irritation only grew.

"Bungboo!"

("Fool!")

He muttered under his breath, glaring at Tashi's carefree attitude.

Despite the tension, the group was ushered toward the lawn, and Sonam quickly began gathering the plastic chairs, his movements hurried and almost frantic as he worked to avoid further embarrassment. The villagers, who had been watching the scene unfold with interest from rooftops and windows, remained curious, their eyes darting between the royal entourage and the chaotic preparations on the lawn.

Sonam, clearly flustered, called out to the onlookers, his voice rising above the murmurs of the village.

"Eka chang ltanmo dultey manok. Songshig, 0Rang rang e last choshik!

("People! Go do your own work! This isn't a fair—get back to your duties!")

He shouted, his face flushed with a mix of exasperation and urgency.

The villagers smirked, exchanging knowing glances, but obediently began to disperse. The peaceful atmosphere of the village returned, though there was still an undercurrent of curiosity lingering in the air as they moved out of view.

Amelia stepped forward, extending her hand to Tashi with a polite smile, her demeanor warm despite the tense atmosphere. Khalid followed suit; his regal presence impossible to ignore. He offered a formal Salaam, his tone carrying the weight of his royal status, though his expression remained composed and neutral.

Ahmed, ever watchful, stood just a few steps behind Khalid, his steely gaze scanning the surroundings with a practiced ease. His focus was unwavering, ensuring that the perimeter remained secure as the group settled.

Tashi, sensing the shift in energy, suddenly dropped his playful demeanor. His grin faded as he bowed slightly, a show of respect that seemed foreign to him in this context. He was no longer the carefree man who had welcomed them with a joke; now, he was fully aware of the weight of the guests before him.

From the window of the house, Dolma's eyes widened in surprise. She had never seen her husband act in such a way before—always brash, always relaxed. But now, here he was, humbling himself before royalty. The transformation was evident, and she couldn't help but stare in stunned silence, her hands frozen mid-task.

It was clear that this moment, this unexpected meeting, had already begun to shift the dynamics in ways that no one could have anticipated.

Moments later, Sonam returned, moving with purpose as he carried a luxurious new carpet draped over his shoulder. His eyes darted between the guests and the lawn, and with a decisive motion, he rolled the carpet out in the center, instantly transforming the humble space into something more refined. Plush silk pillows followed, arranged in a semi-circle. With each careful adjustment, the scene took on a touch of elegance, an inviting seating area that belied the simplicity of the surroundings.

Sonam stepped back, surveying his work with a satisfied nod, before heading inside. He returned moments later, this time with a tray of high-end crockery. At the center of the tray sat an ornate kettle of steaming tea, surrounded by gleaming sugar cubes in a delicate bowl. The sight was enough to make Dolma, standing near the window, pause. Her face softened with appreciation as she watched Sonam's meticulous attention to detail. He was handling the hospitality like a true master.

As she handed him the last of the serving dishes, she leaned in closer, her voice soft with gratitude.

"Thukji che, kaga ley."

("Thank you, brother.")

Dolma murmured, her voice barely above a whisper.

"Rang na phantoks ma srantey tangs. Nerang med pinna na las khong dubches midug pin."

("You've truly been a help. I don't know what I would've done without you.")

Sonam's smile was warm, his reassuring gaze never leaving Dolma's face.

"Chang mirak pa Dolma. Rang Ranga maphan na sua phanin."

("It's nothing, Dolma. Family always stands together.")

He replied, his voice filled with sincerity.

Dolma smiled back, a flicker of pride in her expression, though it was tinged with nerves.

The setup now looked almost regal, the combination of the carpet, pillows, and tea service standing in stark contrast to the rugged backdrop of the Ladakhi valley.

Together, they carried the tea service out to the guests, placing the items with care, a mix of reverence and humility in every movement. The security personnel, respectful as always, were served their own tea at the edge of the lawn, positioned just far enough to offer the group privacy without leaving them entirely unattended.

Amelia settled comfortably onto one of the silk pillows, lifting her teacup with a gracious nod to Dolma.

"Thank you for your hospitality," she said, her voice smooth and warm.

"We appreciate it."

Dolma, visibly flattered yet slightly overwhelmed by the attention, gave a grateful smile, nodding in acknowledgment.

Before the conversation could continue, Khalid broke the silence, his tone firm but measured as he spoke directly to Tashi.

"So, tell us about this tattoo."

The words hung in the air for a moment, but before Tashi could respond, Ahmed stepped forward. He held up a hand to stop him, casting a sharp look at Sonam before turning back to Tashi.

"You're speaking to His Highness," Ahmed stated plainly, his voice cold and commanding.

"Choose your words carefully."

Tension thickened the air, and for a brief moment, the peaceful setting seemed to darken. But Amelia, sensing the rising strain, gently placed a hand on Ahmed's shoulder. Her smile was warm, a subtle yet clear invitation to ease the tension.

"Please, don't mind our friend," she said, her voice soft and reassuring.

"Go on..."

Tashi hesitated for a moment, then nodded, his gaze shifting to the distant valley as if searching for something. The air around him seemed quiet, his mind seemingly reaching back into memories long buried.

"This tattoo,"

Tashi began, his voice distant as if recalling a faraway time,

"it's the one I gave to Shiva, my friend. He's from the snow-covered mountain regions of Kashmir. We shared a place in New Delhi once, when we were in our early twenties, back when I was just starting as a tattoo student. Those were good days. We had so much fun back then. I haven't heard from him in years now."

He paused, his eyes flickering as a flood of memories washed over him. Sonam, standing off to the side, was clearly intrigued, watching with rapt attention. Dolma, still in the background, listened intently, her curiosity piqued by the mention of this mysterious figure from Tashi's past.

"Shiva?"

Amelia asked, her voice curious but gentle, her eyebrows lifting slightly in interest.

Tashi nodded, his eyes softening as he answered.

"Yes, like Lord Shiva in Hinduism,"

He explained, as if the connection were obvious.

Khalid's skepticism was apparent as he leaned forward, his gaze sharp.

"Do you have a picture of him?"

Tashi nodded slowly, standing up and moving inside his house. He returned a few moments later, holding a photo album in his hands. He flipped through the pages until he found the ones he was looking for—two photos in particular: one of the tattoo he had drawn on Shiva's arm and another of the two of them together in the tattoo studio in New Delhi. Tashi handed the photos to Ahmed, who was standing beside Khalid. Ahmed passed them along to Khalid and Amelia, who examined them closely.

The image of Shiva's tattoo was intricate, detailed, a work of art in itself. But it was the eyes in the photos that drew their attention—the eyes that seemed to hold a story, a secret. The briefest flashback of Volk's eyes in Siberia flickered in their minds, the connection sudden and unsettling.

Tashi continued, his voice growing quieter, as if lost in the memory.

"I remember asking him why he wanted such an intricate tattoo. He looked at me like I couldn't see something he was seeing. He told me he was a Sagittarius and had always felt a deep connection to the bow and arrow, something that had been with him since childhood."

The moment became still. The breeze, cool and gentle, rustled the leaves of the nearby trees, adding a subtle rhythm to the heavy silence that now hung between them. Khalid and Amelia exchanged a glance, their eyes reflecting the same fleeting thought—a vision of an arrow cutting through the tiger's skin in Siberia.

Amelia's voice broke the quiet, her curiosity shining through.

"Tell us everything about him..."

Tashi's gaze wandered once more, his thoughts drifting back to that time.

"He was studying business," he said, his voice filled with a distant affection.

"Intelligent, ambitious—he wanted to make something big of himself. He loved solving problems, always had a pure heart, loved people... he was full of life."

As Tashi spoke, it was as though he were transported back to those days in New Delhi, recalling the nights spent in a bustling neighborhood full of dreams, laughter, and the quiet comfort of a friendship that felt destined. But now, in the present, his voice held a note of melancholy, a longing for the days long gone.

***

The golden light of the evening stretched across the busy streets, casting long, elongated shadows as the sun sank lower, nearing its descent. The vibrant energy of Connaught Place, with its throngs of people and honking cars, blended with the air of a city that was never quite ready to slow down. But amidst the rush, two young men broke the rhythm of the evening, sprinting down the sidewalk, laughter ringing out through the crowded streets.

Tashi and Shiva, side by side, weaved through the pedestrians with carefree abandon, their sneakers slapping against the pavement, the wind whipping through their hair. The air was thick with the scent of street food, but it was their energy that dominated the scene—wild, untamed, and exhilarating. Behind them, the sound of heavy footsteps grew louder, and a voice, desperate and out of breath, called out.

"Ruko"

("Stop!")

The sweaty cop in uniform, struggling to keep up with their pace, puffed his chest as he tried to close the gap. But Shiva, with the speed and agility of a man who knew the streets too well, slowed just enough to glance over his shoulder, a mischievous glint in his eyes.

He raised the beer bottle in his hand in a mock toast, his grin wide and playful.

"Oye thulle, le pee le"

("Yo! constable, come, have a sip!")

Shiva taunted, his voice carrying a carefree mockery.

The cop, breathless and red-faced, staggered forward, his steps faltering with every desperate movement. He was close now—close enough that Shiva could almost feel the officer's ragged breath on his back. But in a moment of pure mischief, Shiva turned on his heel and, with a burst of energy, dashed off again, his laughter echoing through the street.

The cop was left behind, leaning heavily against a streetlight, hands on his knees as he caught his breath. With a final, defeated wave, he muttered something under his breath, his futile pursuit at an end. The chaos of the city resumed around them, but for a brief moment, it had been just the three of them—two friends, running wild, and a cop who couldn't keep up.

The pulsating beat of music wrapped around Tashi and Shiva as they stepped into the dimly lit night club, the atmosphere alive with the sound of laughter and chatter. They entered side by side, laughing and holding onto each other like old friends who had nothing but good times ahead. The club's neon lights bounced off their faces as they made their way through the crowd. Shiva, tall and strikingly handsome, moved with a quiet confidence that drew the eyes of those nearby. His presence was magnetic, and as he walked, he could feel the glances of the onlookers, their curiosity and admiration obvious.

They found a spot near the bar, the hum of conversation and music swirling around them. Both grabbed a cold Budweiser, the chill of the bottle against their palms a welcome contrast to the warmth of the crowded club. The clink of glass bottles echoed as they tapped them together in a casual toast.

Tashi, still grinning from their earlier adventure, leaned in toward Shiva.

"Yaar policewale ne tujhe almost pakad hi liya tha"

("Man, the cop almost had you,")

He teased.

Shiva chuckled, taking a long sip from his bottle.

"Almost. Mujhe pata tha ki uska kuch nahi ho sakta. Who sahi se saans toh le nahi paa raha tha"

("Almost. I knew he didn't stand a chance. Dude could barely breathe")

He replied, his voice laced with amusement.

Their laughter blended into the cacophony of the club, but a subtle shift in the room caught Tashi's attention. He noticed two girls across the room, their heads turning occasionally in Shiva's direction. They were whispering and giggling, exchanging glances while stealing quick looks at Shiva. One of the girls, dressed in a pink dress, seemed particularly intrigued.

Tashi, his eyes gleaming with mischief, nudged Shiva in the ribs.

"Who ladki jo pink dress mein hai, kaafi der se ghoore ja rahi hai"

("That girl in pink has been eyeing you for a while now.")

Shiva, with a nonchalant shrug, glanced over at the girls.

"Hmmm.. mujhe pata hai"

("Hmmm... I know.")

Tashi raised an eyebrow.

"So?"

Shiva shrugged again, unfazed.

"Nah... not my type. She probably just wants a quick fling."

Tashi, ever the optimist, grinned.

"Arey aisa mat soch, mujhe toh who kaafi cool lag rahi hai"

("Oh, come on, don't judge! She looks pretty chill to me.")

Shiva, now a little tipsy, gestured toward the girl in pink, who quickly looked away, pretending she hadn't been watching. He smirked.

"Dekh! Who khud toh tey nahi kar paa rhi ki kya chahiye"

("Look at her! She can't even make up her mind. So confused.")

The girl turned her eyes away, flustered, her cheeks turning pink as she fidgeted nervously. Shiva and Tashi shared a laugh, but the moment was abruptly interrupted by a tap on Shiva's shoulder. He turned around to come face-to-face with a towering, intimidating figure—a man who had been trying to impress the girl himself. He held Shiva from his collar.

The man's voice was thick with anger as he spoke, his words dripping with hostility.

"Oye ke samja se tu, uspe ungli dikha ke? Main tanne dekh raya tha, samja?"

("Who do you think you are, pointing at her like that? I've been watching you, huh?")

Shiva's confidence evaporated in an instant. His face drained of color, and for a split second, he froze, unable to respond. His eyes widened, his breath catching in his chest. The intensity of the man's anger overwhelmed him, and a wave of panic hit him like a freight train. His breathing became shallow and rapid as his body froze in place.

Tashi, ever perceptive, sensed the change in the air. Without missing a beat, he stepped in, placing a protective hand on Shiva's shoulder. His movements were fluid, almost theatrical, as he leaned in and spoke with exaggerated sweetness.

"Oh, bro! What girl? We're... you know... we're a couple,"

Tashi said, his voice dripping with faux innocence.

He gestured between himself and Shiva with a flourish, leaning in further and batting his eyelashes dramatically.

"Don't mind us, bro. We were just... chilling!"

The large man recoiled in disgust, his face contorting as if he'd just smelled something foul. He pushed Shiva away, sneering in utter disdain.

"Hain? Bhen ke lodo bahar nikalo"

"Yuck! What the—?! Get out, you two... assholes!")

He barked; his voice venomous as he turned away in disgust.

Tashi quickly wrapped his arm around Shiva's shoulders, guiding him away from the confrontation. He shot the man a dismissive glance before leading Shiva out of the club, the cool night air hitting them as they stepped outside.

Once they were out of the club, Tashi glanced over at Shiva, noticing that his friend was still visibly shaken. Shiva's chest rose and fell quickly, and his eyes remained wide, as if still processing the encounter.

Tashi's voice softened, his usual teasing tone replaced by genuine concern.

"Hey... you okay? What just happened back there?"

Shiva, still rattled, stared blankly ahead.

"I... I don't know. I've never been treated like that. Was I... was I just bullied?"

His voice was barely above a whisper, as though he were still trying to make sense of it all.

Tashi nodded slowly, his face serious for a moment.

"Yeah... kind of. He's just an idiot with muscles. But you're alright now."

Shiva took a shaky breath, still lost in the memory of the confrontation.

"He was massive, I don't know. I froze up."

Tashi gave him a small, reassuring smile, clapping him gently on the back.

"Leave it. Chal tere design pe kaam karte hain"

("Leave it. Let's go work on your design.")

With that, the tension seemed to ease a little. Shiva's breathing slowed, and as they walked into the night, the weight of the moment seemed to lift. They eventually arrived at a small, warmly lit tattoo studio. The familiar hum of tattoo machines and the quiet ambiance of the place grounded Shiva. As he stepped inside, the buzzing of the machines seemed to steady his nerves. The calm of the studio was a welcome relief from the chaos of the night, and as he exhaled deeply, he allowed himself to relax.

The tattoo studio was tucked away on a bustling market street in New Delhi, a modest space where the hum of the busy marketplace outside merged with the steady, rhythmic sound of a tattoo needle. The air was thick with the scent of incense, mingling with the distant calls of street vendors and the rich aroma of sizzling street food.

Tashi, young and focused, leaned over his work with a concentration that left no room for distractions. His hands moved deftly, the needle punctuating the skin of his client with a precision that belied his years. The tattoo taking shape on Shiva's arm was intricate—an image of Lord Shiva, draped in a tiger's skin, his hair tied atop his head, his third eye wide open, and poised to release an arrow from a taut bow. The design seemed to pulse with a life of its own, the ink glistening under Tashi's skilled touch as if the god himself might step out from the skin.

Shiva, the man in the chair, clenched his jaw, his breath sharp and uneven as the needle continued its work. His face was shadowed, but his icy, intense eyes flashed with each jolt of pain.

"Enough, bro,"

Shiva groaned; his voice strained.

"You said it would only take a few hours. It's been fourteen hours already!"

Tashi chuckled softly, his focus unwavering as he wiped away a streak of ink. His voice, thick with a Ladakhi accent, was laced with amusement.

"Relax, bro! Art takes time—especially this kind of art. This is no ordinary tattoo."

Shiva grimaced, wincing as the needle pressed deeper into his skin.

"Easy for you to say! You're not the one bleeding and sitting here."

He glanced up at Tashi, the hint of a smile playing beneath his pained expression.

"And you said I would need just a snack break,"

Shiva continued, voice tinged with both frustration and laughter.

Tashi laughed in return, wiping away the ink and admiring his progress.

"A snack break? You're from Kashmir; I thought you would have the endurance of a snow leopard! Where's that famous grit of yours, Shiva?"

Shiva's grin widened despite the discomfort.

"It's here. Trust me, if you weren't my friend, I would have kicked you out that window by now."

He gestured toward the window, where the street outside was a whirlwind of activity—vendors shouting their wares, customers haggling, and the rich, spicy scent of food filling the air.

Tashi smirked, his hands still steady.

"Then it's a good thing we're friends. Besides, if it's worth it, it's worth the pain. This is a once-in-a-lifetime piece, Shiva."

Shiva let out a half-hearted laugh, but it was quickly followed by another groan as the needle dug in once more.

"Once in a lifetime... behanchod dobara nahi karva raha main but seriously, how much longer"

("Once in a lifetime... You got that right. Never doing this again. But seriously, how much longer?")

Tashi paused, taking a moment to assess the progress of the tattoo. His fingers gently wiped away the ink and blood, revealing the intricate layers of Shiva's likeness.

"We're close. Maybe another hour if you can take it. But after this, you'll need to rest up and let your skin heal before we can work on the second part. Your skin's fighting back now."

"Fighting back?", Shiva sighed, his voice tinged with a mix of humor and exhaustion.

"Great, even my skin's tired."

He looked down at the tattoo, transfixed despite the pain.

"You know,", Shiva said, his voice quieter now, almost introspective,

"Jab se mujhe hosh hai, main yahi chahta hoon. The bow and arrow... it's a part of me. Felt that way since I was a kid. I guess it's because I'm a Sagittarius or something. Symbol of a warrior, maybe?"

("I've wanted this for as long as I can remember. The bow and arrow... it's a part of me. Felt that way since I was a kid. I guess it's because I'm a Sagittarius or something. Symbol of a warrior, maybe?")

Tashi nodded, intrigued by his friend's words.

"It suits your name. Now that you mention you're a Sagittarius... it's like it was made for you."

Shiva grinned, the pain momentarily forgotten.

"Yeah, well, I'll look the part, but if Shanaya asks, I'll tell her it was painless. Let's keep my suffering between us."

Tashi smirked, his hands never faltering. He gave Shiva a conspiratorial wink.

"Of course, your secret's safe. But you'll owe me more than just a chai for this."

Shiva laughed, though the sound was muffled by exhaustion.

"Done. When I'm successful, I'll buy you something you need but can't afford. And promise me one thing."

Tashi met his friend's intense gaze, his expression softening.

"Anything, bro."

Shiva's voice grew serious, carrying a weight that contrasted sharply with the light-hearted banter from before.

"I'm leaving next week for my job, so it's on you to finish the second part of this tattoo. I don't know when I'll get the time again. But wherever you are, I'll find you."

There was a quiet pause. Tashi's hands rested gently on Shiva's arm, the moment settling between them. Tashi, moved by the gravity of Shiva's words, gave a small nod.

"Deal. I'm framing this tattoo anyway. It's my first major work."

They shared a look—a silent understanding passing between them. Life's paths might soon pull them in different directions, but for now, this moment was theirs.

Outside, the sounds of the market began to fade into the background as Tashi's meticulous hands finished the last details of the tattoo. The design now looked fierce, alive with energy, as though Lord Shiva himself might leap from Shiva's arm at any moment. Tashi wiped the tattoo clean one final time, stepping back to admire his work.

"There you go,"

Tashi said, a sense of pride in his voice.

"Finished for now. Your Shiva is ready."

Shiva stared down at his arm, his eyes wide with admiration, pride, and a trace of awe.

"It's perfect. Thanks, Tashi."

Tashi smiled, reaching for his camera. He snapped a picture of the tattoo, then handed the camera to his colleague before sitting down beside Shiva.

"Alright, now say cheese..."

The studio, filled with the quiet hum of accomplishment and the distant sounds of the market outside, faded as Tashi and Shiva shared a moment of connection—one that would endure beyond the pain and the ink.

***

The grand hall of the King's palace was bathed in the soft, fading light of early evening. The air was thick with the weight of history, the high ceilings echoing with the soft murmur of unseen servants moving in the background. Long shadows stretched across the marble floors, the intricate tapestries on the walls whispering secrets of forgotten times. The room, both regal and somber, seemed to hold its breath in the presence of power.

At the far end of the hall, the KING stood, his back to the ornate windows that framed the dying sun. His posture was regal, yet there was an underlying tension in his stillness, as though he were a predator waiting for the right moment to strike. He turned slowly, his gaze settling on the two Arab bodyguards who had just entered, their movements deliberate, their expressions unreadable.

The bodyguards bowed low, their faces shadowed by the flickering light of the candles that adorned the room. Their silence was a mark of respect, but also of the seriousness that hung in the air.

The KING's voice broke the quiet, commanding yet calm, the words carrying the weight of a ruler's expectation.

"Qabla an nugādira ghadan, akhbirūnī bi-kulli mā taʿrifūnahu ʿan hādhā... Volk."

("Before we leave tomorrow, tell me everything you know about this... Volk.")

He said, his gaze was steady and piercing.

One of the bodyguards stepped forward, his head bowed in deference, his eyes never meeting the KING's. His tone was measured, careful. He began

"Yā Ṣāḥib al-Jalālah, kāna min shibhi al-mustaḥīl al-ʿuthūr ʿalā ayy shakhṣin yaʿrifuhu ḥaqqan. Aʿḍāʾ ʿiṣābatih... jamīʿuhum mātū. Wa maʿa dhālik, kāna hunāka rajul wāḥid — shakhṣun qābalahu marratan wāḥidah faqaṭ. Waṣafa Volk bi-annahu kāna waḥshiyyan. Quwwa min quwā al-ṭabīʿah, lā akthar wa lā aqall."

("Your Highness, it was nearly impossible to find anyone who truly knew him. His gang members... they're all dead. However, there was one man—someone who encountered him only once. He... he described Volk as animalistic. A true force of nature.")

The KING's expression remained unreadable, but there was a flicker of something in his eyes—a spark of interest, perhaps, or something darker. His lips barely parted as he spoke again, his voice low, but carrying the sharpness of a man who did not let things slip past him.

"Waḥshiyy, taqūl?"

("Animalistic, you say?")

He mused, his words trailing off as if savoring the thought.

("Hmmm...")

The tension in the room thickened, the weight of the moment hanging between the KING and his bodyguard. The flickering candlelight seemed to pause, holding its breath in the quiet before the storm. The KING, ever the enigma, waited for more, as though his next move depended on the answers he would receive.

***

The frigid streets of the small Siberian town stretched out before the two bodyguards: their breaths visible in the biting cold air. The sky was an ashen gray, thick clouds swirling ominously overhead as the town seemed to sink further into twilight, the dimming light doing little to warm the weathered buildings and frost-covered streets. Everything about this place felt abandoned, as though the cold itself had claimed both the town and its people, leaving only the remnants of life.

Bundled up tightly in thick coats, scarves, and gloves, the bodyguards trudged through the town, their steps crunching on the hard snow beneath them. They stopped every so often, trying to engage the locals—fishermen, shopkeepers, and passersby—but each question was met with evasiveness, averted gazes, and uncomfortable silence. It was clear no one wanted to talk about the man they sought—the infamous Volk.

BODYGUARD #2, with a hardened edge to his voice, approached a passerby, his eyes narrowing as he pressed for answers.

"Do you know anyone who's met him? The Volk?"

The elderly woman, her back hunched with age and her weather-beaten face covered in a veil of snow, glanced up from beneath her heavy scarf. She didn't hesitate, her voice soft but firm as she pointed down a narrow, snow-covered path.

"You want Randy," she said.

"He's the only one who might know."

The bodyguards exchanged a brief, knowing look before following her direction, their boots leaving deep impressions in the fresh snow as they made their way through the winding streets. As they approached a rougher neighborhood on the outskirts of town, the air grew even colder, the buildings older and more decrepit. They stopped in front of a dilapidated structure, its windows boarded up and the door crooked on its hinges. A small boy was playing in the snow outside, his face pale and freckled beneath a woolen cap.

BODYGUARD #1 eyed the boy and asked,

"Is this Randy's place?"

The little boy looked up, a trace of hesitation before he nodded eagerly.

"Yes. That's Randy's house."

The bodyguards exchanged another glance, a signal to proceed. They marched up to the door, their heavy boots crunching on the snow as they knocked loudly, their fists making a firm, authoritative sound against the wood. There was a long pause before the door creaked open, revealing the imposing figure of RANDY.

He was a hulking man, his muscles thick and undefined beneath his worn jacket. A faint scar ran across his nose, the mark of a past encounter that had left its permanent reminder. His eyes widened momentarily when he saw the armed men standing at his doorstep, his posture instantly stiffening, like a cornered animal.

BODYGUARD #2, stepping forward with an air of authority, spoke first.

"Hello, Randy. We're here to ask you a few questions. Hope you'll cooperate."

Randy glanced down at the guns strapped to their sides, his gaze flickering between them and the door behind him. After a moment of hesitation, he stepped aside, gesturing for them to come in. His face held no welcome, but it was clear he wasn't about to turn them away.

Inside, the living room was dimly lit, the shadows in the corners of the room stretching long across the floor. The room was cluttered, an assortment of old furniture, half-drunk bottles of liquor, and mismatched items scattered around. The air was thick with the scent of stale smoke, and the warmth from the small stove in the corner didn't do much to fight off the cold that seemed to seep into the very walls.

RANDY sat across from the bodyguards, his massive form almost swallowing the chair he sat in. His hands were folded tightly in his lap, his eyes darting nervously between the men. His posture was tense, every inch of him alert and wary.

BODYGUARD #1 didn't waste time, his tone flat but insistent.

"We need to know everything you remember about Volk."

RANDY's gaze shifted downward, his fingers tapping lightly on the arm of the chair as if to steady himself. His voice came out low, almost a whisper, but the words were clear.

"He's... he's a freak, that one," he said, his voice quivering slightly.

"Calm yet cold, deadly. Like he has no soul, no emotions."

His eyes glazed over as if the memory of Volk haunted him.

"Like he's... not even human."

He hesitated, his fingers unconsciously grazing the scar across his nose, the painful reminder of his brief, violent encounter with the man they were hunting.

"This is what he gave me," Randy added, his voice suddenly sharp, like a knife cutting through the air. His hand, now trembling, pointed toward the scar.

The bodyguards watched him closely, their eyes cold and unreadable as the silence between them deepened. Randy shifted uncomfortably, his eyes flickering with a mixture of fear and anger as he relived the moment, but it was clear he was not going to offer more unless pressed. The weight of what he knew hung in the air, the tension palpable.

***

The old factory building on the outskirts of town stood as a crumbling monument to industry's past, its weathered exterior reflecting the rusting machinery within. Inside, the low hum of flickering lights buzzed above a room filled with the sounds of grunting and clanging iron. Men of varying shapes and sizes pushed their bodies to the limit, the air thick with the smell of sweat and raw effort. Some lifted weights, others sparred, all trained with a ferocity borne from a world that had never shown them mercy. This was a place for the hard and the ruthless—an ally to the twin brothers who ran this operation.

Volk entered, flanked by the twin brothers, his presence slicing through the noise like a blade through silk. Cold, calculating eyes scanned the room, briefly glancing over the men, assessing their weaknesses and their strengths. The brothers exchanged a quick look, then gestured to the corner of the gym.

"Stay here," one of the brothers said, his voice low.

"We need them as well for the expedition."

Volk gave a curt nod, his eyes still fixed on the men training. He didn't speak—his silence said enough. The brothers moved toward a set of stairs at the far end of the room, heading up to a glass-enclosed office. From there, they would look over the gym floor, surveying everything like gods on high. Inside the office, a mafia boss stood silhouetted against the fading light. His figure was imposing, his presence even more so, as he turned to greet them.

"Ah, brothers! I've been expecting you," the boss said, spreading his arms wide in a grand gesture of welcome.

The gym buzzed with the sound of weights being slammed against the floor, heavy breathing filling the air, and the clatter of metal reverberating through the vast space. Dust filtered through the high windows, casting long shadows across the exposed beams and pipes overhead. Volk moved through the gym with the same calm he always exuded, unbothered by the noise around him. He was a man apart, his focus singular and absolute.

He walked over to a corner, and removed his coat and shirt with quiet precision, laying them neatly over a bag. Without a glance, he slipped on his headphones and began his workout, his movements slow and controlled. Each rep, each lift was done with a quiet intensity, as if he were in a world of his own, separated from the chaos around him.

But it didn't take long before someone noticed. Randy, a mountain of a man, entered the gym like a storm cloud. His presence loomed over the others, and the room seemed to shrink in size as he moved through it. Arrogance radiated off him, and the gym-goers instinctively stepped aside, eyes lowering in deference. He walked over to a woman in the middle of her set, his eyes lingering on her for a moment before he reached out and slapped her ass.

She flinched, a flicker of anger in her eyes, but said nothing. She quickly moved away, her back stiff, not daring to confront him. Randy smirked, clearly enjoying the power he held over everyone here. He made his way to the bench press next, where two young men were lifting.

"I need this," Randy said, his voice a low growl as he loomed over them, blocking their light.

"Move."

The young men exchanged nervous glances before stepping aside. They didn't want trouble, not with a man like Randy. He set about loading the bar with an absurd amount of weight, his massive hands gripping it with a terrifying ease. As he began his set, his face reddened with effort, sweat pouring down his forehead as he pushed against the weight, grunting with every strained rep. His movements were jerky, unrefined. He struggled to maintain control, but his brute strength pushed him through.

Across the gym, Volk watched quietly, his eyes never leaving Randy. There was no judgment in his gaze, only observation. He had seen men like Randy before—men who relied on sheer force, but lacked the grace that came with true strength. Randy noticed him too.

When Randy finished his set, he wiped his face with a rag and glanced over at Volk. He was breathing heavily, his body still trembling from the strain. Without missing a beat, he walked over to the incline bench, where Volk had set up for his next set. Randy's eyes narrowed as he approached. Volk gives him a skeptical look.

"You think you can outlift me?", Randy sneered.

"Let's see what you've got."

Randy slapped more weight onto the bar with a forceful grunt, his face contorting in a grimace of determination. He gripped the bar, his muscles trembling as he pushed through six difficult reps. His arms shook, his breaths coming in labored gasps, but he somehow managed to finish. Sweat was dripping down his face, and his eyes darted around the room, looking for any sign of admiration, but the other gym-goers were either too nervous or uninterested to pay him any real attention.

Volk, meanwhile, remained unphased. Calmly, he approached the bench. Without a word, he removed some of the excess weight and set the bar to a manageable load. He adjusted everything with a practiced hand, his movements smooth and fluid. His muscles rippled with each precise movement, each rep fluid and controlled. There was no struggle, no tension in his body. He moved through the set, with 20 reps, as if it were effortless.

Randy watched, his jaw tightening. His hands clenched into fists as Volk finished with ease, not even breaking a sweat. His face was set in a scowl, his pride stung by the quiet display of skill.

"Baby Weights. Fucking pussy"

Randy spat, striding over to Volk and yanking his headphones off his head, his voice dripping with mockery.

Volk didn't react. He didn't flinch. His eyes, cold and unyielding, met Randy's. Silence hung in the air between them, thick and palpable. The tension was so heavy, it could have been cut with a knife. Around them, people started to notice, the murmurs and whispers growing louder as the confrontation escalated. Above, the twin brothers watched, their faces betraying nothing but the slightest flicker of concern.

Randy, unwilling to back down, decided to go even further. He added more weight to the bar, his hands shaking as he did so. His face twisted in determination as he pressed the barbell up, each rep shakier than the last. His muscles screamed in protest, but he pushed through, desperate to prove himself. He hardly finished the set with 4 reps, but the struggle was evident.

Volk, unfazed, walked over to the bench once again. Without a word, he reclaimed the space, his movements smooth and effortless. He proceeded with the same weight Randy had just struggled with, and with the grace of a seasoned lifter, he pushed through eight flawless reps. Each movement was deliberate, each breath controlled. The contrast between him and Randy was glaring.

A quiet ripple of laughter spread through the gym. It wasn't loud, but it was enough to make Randy's face turn crimson with anger. He could feel the eyes on him, the judgment in the air. The tension was palpable, but no one dared to speak out loud.

Volk didn't care. He picked up his headphones once more, slipping them back on as the soothing sound of music filled his ears. He continued his workout, focused once more, as if the world around him had ceased to exist.

But Randy wasn't done. Fueled by a mix of rage and embarrassment, he stormed over to Volk, shoving him hard, knocking him off balance. The weight plate dropped with a loud crash.

"You think you're tough?"

Randy growled; his voice laced with venom.

Volk steadied himself, his expression hardening. His gaze locked onto Randy with a chilling intensity, and for a moment, the entire gym seemed to freeze.

With a smooth, almost imperceptible motion, Volk bent down and picked up the dropped weight plate. His eyes never left Randy's, his gaze unwavering, his intent clear. In a blur, he swung the plate with devastating speed, smashing it across Randy's face. Blood sprayed as Randy recoiled in shock, stumbling back.

Before Randy could react, Volk was on him. His fists flew in a flurry of precise, brutal punches. Each blow landed with pinpoint accuracy, the sound of bone meeting flesh filling the gym. Randy hit the floor, dazed and bleeding, but Volk didn't stop. He continued to strike, his blows unrelenting.

The crowd circled around them, horrified but mesmerized by the sheer violence of the scene. The twin brothers rushed down from the balcony, their hands grabbing Volk's arms, pulling him away from the battered Randy. They urged him to stop, but Volk was calm, his breathing steady once more as he stood over his fallen opponent.

The mafia boss emerged from the shadows, his gaze cold and impassive as he looked down at the beaten Randy.

"Get the hell out of here," the mafia boss said, his voice icy.

Randy staggered to his feet, his face bloodied and bruised. His arrogance was gone, replaced by the bitter sting of humiliation. He limped away, not a word escaping his lips.

Volk, on the other hand, remained unaffected. He simply returned to his workout, as though nothing had happened, each lift a silent testament to his unshakable resolve.

***

The grand hall of the King's palace was bathed in the soft glow of candlelight, the high arches of the stone walls casting long shadows across the polished floors. The air was thick with the scent of incense, lingering in the space like a reminder of ancient rituals.

In the center, the KING sat upon his throne, his posture regal but relaxed, his fingers drumming rhythmically on the armrest. His eyes, however, remained fixed on the men before him, who were recounting the details of the brutal confrontation involving Volk.

The KING's advisors stood at attention, their faces passive, their eyes trained on the unfolding conversation. They knew better than to interrupt when their monarch was lost in thought. The room was otherwise still, as if time had momentarily slowed for the momentous tale being shared.

As the final words of the recounting echoed in the hall, the KING remained silent, his gaze distant. He seemed to peer beyond the walls of the room, his mind no doubt painting a picture of the violent scene described to him. His fingers, long and pale, continued their rhythmic tapping, an absentminded gesture that masked the intensity of his thoughts.

Then, after a long pause, the KING leaned forward ever so slightly, his lips parting to release a quiet, thoughtful murmur.

"Ḥayawān"

("An animal,")

He said, his voice low but rich with intrigue, as if savoring the words.

"Madfūʿ bil-gharīza"

("Driven by instinct...")

He fell silent again, as though weighing the meaning of the words, contemplating the nature of the man described. His eyes narrowed, a flicker of a smile tugging at the corner of his mouth. The smile, though faint, carried a sense of satisfaction—a recognition of something more, something primal, in the man known as Volk.

Finally, the KING leaned back in his throne, his expression shifting into something almost imperceptibly pleased. He looked ahead, as though imagining the figure of Volk standing before him. The anticipation was palpable in the air, a thread of excitement weaving through his demeanor as he waited for the day he would meet this enigmatic, merciless figure in person.

***

The evening air was thick with an unsettled tension. The sky above had begun to soften into a twilight hue, casting the world in shades of amber and purple, but outside Tashi's modest home, the atmosphere remained heavy and confused. No one could shake the unsettling feeling that lingered, as though the conversation had only raised more questions than answers.

Shiva, the gentle, anxious man that Tashi knew felt entirely at odds with the ferocious, survival-driven nature of the person they were looking for. Volk's name hung in the air like a whisper of a nightmare—a man whose instincts were sharper than any blade, whose capacity for violence was boundless. The contrast between the two was stark, as if they were discussing entirely different people. Sonam and Dolma listened carefully, their faces etched with confusion, their eyes moving from one speaker to the next, trying to make sense of the pieces that didn't fit together.

Khalid stood by the edge of the lawn, looking out at the faint outlines of the mountains, his mind clearly racing. He glanced between Tashi and the others, trying to reconcile what had been said with the image of the person they thought they knew. The conflict was evident, and it gnawed at him.

Beside him, Amelia stood silently, her arms folded across her chest. The disappointment in her eyes was undeniable, the frustration of their long journey, the dead ends, the unanswered questions, all catching up with her. She had hoped for clarity, but instead, they were no closer to understanding.

Khalid's voice broke the silence, laced with frustration.

"I'm not sure if it's the same man," he said, his words heavy with uncertainty.

"We're anyway going to meet this man tomorrow. If there's a connection, we'll let you know."

Amelia, always the diplomat, nodded in agreement, offering a polite smile that didn't quite reach her eyes.

"Thank you for the warm hospitality."

Sonam, sensing the tension, stepped forward, his expression earnest.

"No problem, your highness. Rest assured, Tashi didn't make this up."

His words were firm, infused with a quiet conviction.

Khalid let out a long, frustrated sigh, running his hands through his hair.

"No. I can see that he did that tattoo, but maybe we got the sketch wrong. Perhaps it's something more like this or maybe drawn by someone else as well...," he gestured vaguely, his frustration evident in the vague hand movement.

The conversation seemed to hit a standstill, and the group began to drift toward their cars. Outside, the air had turned crisp, and the sun began its slow descent behind the mountains, casting a golden glow over the landscape. The warmth of the day contrasted sharply with the tension that hung in the air, thick with unspoken thoughts.

Khalid and Amelia slipped into their car, the sound of the engine rumbling to life filling the silence. Ahmed, standing by the door, leaned in to speak to the prince. Khalid whispered something in his ear, and Ahmed nodded, understanding the weight of the moment. Without a word, Ahmed went to the trunk, retrieving a briefcase that gleamed under the fading light. The leather was smooth, new, and sturdy—a quiet promise of something important.

He handed the briefcase to Tashi, his expression serious. Tashi's eyes flickered down at the case, uncertainty flickering across his face. He nodded gratefully, exchanging a brief but heartfelt look with Ahmed, his silent thanks carrying more meaning than words ever could.

With a final nod, Ahmed turned away and returned to his car. The convoy began to move, the tires kicking up dust as they rolled down the winding road, the distant mountains fading into the backdrop of the evening sky. Tashi stood still, watching the caravan as it disappeared into the horizon, the weight of the briefcase still heavy in his hands.

Inside Tashi's modest home, the atmosphere shifted, settling into something warmer, yet filled with a deep, quiet intensity. The soft glow of the dimming evening light spilled across the room, casting long shadows over the simple furnishings that filled the small space. A sense of serenity lingered in the air, but it was not without its undercurrent of tension.

Tashi's daughter, fragile and delicate, sat in her wheelchair in the corner of the room. Her frail frame was a stark contrast to the brightness in her eyes. Despite her evident weakness, there was an undeniable spark of life in her gaze, a light that brightened even more as her father entered. She smiled up at him, her expression radiant in its innocence.

Tashi entered with the briefcase in hand, his face drawn tight with confusion and curiosity. He approached his daughter, but before he could speak, Sonam moved closer, carefully unfastening the latch of the briefcase. As the lid was lifted, the room seemed to hold its breath.

Inside, neatly stacked bundles of cash filled the case, each one tightly wrapped and perfectly arranged. The sight was overwhelming. Sonam's hand shook as he reached down to touch the edges of the notes, his eyes wide with disbelief. The reality of the moment began to settle in, heavy and undeniable.

For a few seconds, time seemed to slow. Tashi, Sonam, and Dolma stood still, their minds trying to process what was before them. It wasn't just money—it was a lifeline. A possibility. Tears welled up in Tashi's eyes, the weight of it all becoming too much to bear. He glanced over at his daughter, her tiny hands clasped in her lap, unaware of the enormity of the situation but still offering him that gentle smile.

Dolma, her voice barely above a whisper, broke the silence.

"Dikpa Tashi. Ta mangstey mangpo song."

("Tashi... it's enough. It's more than enough.")

The words hung in the air, and Tashi's face softened, breaking into a mixture of disbelief and profound relief. His emotions, which had been building up all day, finally cracked open. He looked down at the cash, then back at Sonam and Dolma, his voice thick with emotion as he spoke.

"Terewey...na goshes chalak chig khyongad zerarak pin ba..."

("That idiot... he said he'd buy me something I desperately needed....")

A choked laugh escaped his throat, and he wiped at the tears that had begun to fall freely down his face. His eyes drifted once again to his daughter, who looked up at him with innocent curiosity, completely unaware of how close they had come to losing her.

Tashi's face softened even more as he gently reached out and took her hand in his, his voice soft, barely a whisper.

"Chang cha manok hai, Gyala nok...."

("You'll be fine now....")

Sonam quietly closed the briefcase, his own eyes glistening with unshed tears. He placed a comforting hand on Tashi's shoulder, silently offering support. Dolma stepped forward next, wrapping her arms around Tashi in a warm, silent embrace. In that moment, the weight of their struggle seemed to lift, just for a brief second, as they all shared a quiet moment of relief and gratitude.

The scene lingered; the air thick with the unspoken connection between them. Slowly, the light outside continued to fade, the last rays of the sun slipping below the mountains. The soft, golden light that filtered through the window seemed almost like a blessing, casting its gentle warmth over the room, the warmth of hope, and the promise of a better tomorrow.

As Tashi pressed his forehead to his daughter's, the world outside fell into silence, and for the first time in a long while, Tashi's heart felt light, filled with a newfound sense of peace and gratitude.

Where the Silence Lives

A desolate silence stretches across the snow-covered expanse of Siberia, the landscape frozen beneath a blanket of white. The light of the setting sun casts a soft golden glow over the endless snowfields, the sky painted with hues of fading warmth as the night edges closer. The crisp air bites sharply, carrying the weight of a solitude that has stood the test of time. Here, miles from civilization, the world feels suspended in an ancient stillness.

Amidst the vastness of the frozen wilderness, a solitary wooden cabin stands stoic, nestled against a backdrop of towering pine trees. Its weathered exterior, a testament to the harsh elements, seems like a small defiance against the overwhelming vastness of nature. This is Volk's fortress, a place untouched by the trappings of civilization, where the wild reigns supreme, and silence is its eternal companion.

Two wolves, lean and formidable, move with ease across the property. One's sleek fur blends into the snow while other's a sharp contrast, their movements fluid and purposeful. Their ears twitch at every sound, every shift in the wind. Their eyes, sharp and watchful, scan the environment, exuding an unspoken calmness that comes from living in tune with the land.

Nearby, a small pack of Siberian huskies rests beside a weathered wooden sled. The dogs are poised, their bodies a mixture of relaxation and readiness, alert yet patient. They are at home here in the wild, their spirits intertwined with the harsh beauty of this desolate land. The darkness of night creeps closer, but the stillness of the scene remains, as if frozen in time, unbothered by the encroaching world beyond.

Inside the cabin, the faint glow of a cigar flickers in the dim light, casting brief shadows that dance across the walls. Volk stands near the frost-covered window, his thick leather coat wrapped tightly around him, blending seamlessly into the rugged surroundings. His gaze is fixed on the snowy horizon, his eyes narrowed, watching as the world beyond the cabin shifts in subtle ways. The tranquility of his expression is deceiving, a calm that hides a sharp, ever-present readiness—an instinct born from years spent in the underbelly of the world, where danger is always near.

He takes a slow drag from his cigar, the smoke swirling in the cold air before drifting lazily upward. As he exhales, his breath forms a cloud in the freezing room, merging with the mist of the cigar's smoke. Every muscle in his body is taut, poised as if waiting for something he knows is coming.

Then, the silence breaks.

A distant hum, faint at first but unmistakable, cuts through the stillness of the wilderness. The rhythmic thrum of helicopters grows steadily louder, the noise breaking the natural harmony of the land. Volk's grip tightens around the cigar, his focus sharpening, his body already reacting. His wolves, resting a few feet away, stir in response, their ears flicking, their senses alert.

The huskies, lounging by the sled, suddenly spring into action. Their ears prick, eyes wide with attention, as they snap into readiness. They know what the sound means.

Moments later, three military-grade helicopters break through the tree line, their dark shapes cutting the sky with precision. They circle above, a deadly dance, before descending toward the gates of the property with coordinated grace.

Outside, the wolves move instinctively toward the boundary of the property. Low growls rumble deep within their chests, their powerful bodies tensed, ready for whatever approach these intruders might bring. The huskies join them, aligning themselves in a protective line, unwavering and stoic. Their eyes are locked on the approaching helicopters, every muscle in their bodies coiled and ready to spring into action. The land, the wolves, and the huskies are all watching, waiting, as the noise of the helicopters fills the air, louder now, and the tension between man and nature hangs heavy.

The helicopters touch down, their powerful rotors whipping the snow into a frenzy, creating swirling eddies that dance in the cold air. The gusts of wind that follow blur the sharp edges of the landscape, momentarily obscuring the figures below. From the first two choppers, armed guards disembark, their black tactical gear contrasting starkly with the white, frozen expanse. Their movements are fluid, synchronized, and cautious—each step measured, their eyes scanning for any sign of threat. The guards approach the third helicopter, where a more dignified figure emerges.

An older man, dressed in a royal military coat, steps out. His bearing is dignified, his posture stiff yet seasoned with the weight of experience. His eyes, sharp and calculating, take in the environment with the precision of someone accustomed to the nuances of power and control. Behind him, Khalid, Jason and Amelia emerge from the helicopter, flanked by the ever-watchful guards. The tension is palpable among the men in black, their eyes darting warily to the side where the wolves stand, unmoving yet clearly alert. The air seems to thicken with every breath.

The cabin door creaks open behind them, breaking the tension for a moment. Volk steps out onto the porch, his movements calm but purposeful. The faintest wisp of smoke trails from the remnants of his cigar, now discarded. His coat, heavy and worn, rustles softly against the biting wind as he approaches the edge of the porch. Beside him, his white wolf, Yuki, steps forward. The creature's fur gleams in the fading light, its presence both a comfort and a warning. Yuki stands tall, eyes focused, his posture regal yet prepared for action at a moment's notice.

As the royal party slowly approaches the cabin, the guards' glances flicker nervously between the wolves and the dogs. Their unease is evident—unsure of whether the animals are part of the welcome or a silent threat, their instincts telling them to remain alert.

Volk stands still for a moment, his eyes meeting the group with a quiet understanding. He raises a hand, and the tension in the air shifts slightly. At his signal, the dogs fall silent, their gaze never leaving the visitors. Yuki, always close to his side, remains poised, watching them intently with his piercing blue eyes.

Ahmed, the most apprehensive of the group, steps forward with a cautious glance toward Yuki. The wolf's gaze follows him like a shadow, unwavering and unblinking. Volk notices the shift in Ahmed's demeanor. Without a word, he reaches down, patting Yuki on the head in a subtle, almost imperceptible gesture. Yuki's posture relaxes, though he doesn't stray far, his eyes still fixed on the group before him. The silence between the two parties lingers for a moment longer, the snow now the only sound around them, heavy and undisturbed.

The visitors step into Volk's humble cabin, the door creaking softly behind them as they enter. The space is small, yet it feels like a refuge from the harsh world outside. The fire crackles steadily in the stone hearth, casting a warm, golden light that dances across the room, softening the edges of the otherwise utilitarian furnishings. The cabin is sparse, its walls lined with animal pelts, the remnants of hunts that have kept Volk alive during the brutal winters that seem to stretch endlessly across this frozen wilderness. These pelts are more than just decoration—they are the badges of survival, the marks of a life lived at the edge of the world.

The King takes in the rustic charm of the cabin with quiet reverence, his gaze drifting across the room, noting the simplicity, yet the comfort it provides in its own way. There's a reverence in his eyes, not just for the shelter but for the man who built it, and for the sacrifices that must have been made to survive in such isolation.

He speaks softly, his voice sincere, and there is a weight to his words that carries the magnitude of the debt he feels.

King *(softly, with sincerity):*

"Thank you, Volk. Not only my family but my kingdom is indebted to you. You saved our children. This debt can never be repaid. I came here to express my gratitude to you personally."

Volk regards the King for a moment, his expression unreadable. His nod is respectful but without embellishment—no grand gestures, no warmth that could be mistaken for familiarity. His eyes are steady, and though he acknowledges the King's words, there is a clear distance in his gaze—a remoteness that transcends the physical space between them. It's as though Volk is already miles away, in a place that only he knows, a place that this encounter cannot touch.

Ahmed (with a warm tone, introducing the royal party):

"Volk, I present to you our King, the prince and his friends. They owe you, their lives."

Volk acknowledges the King and youngsters with a brief, almost imperceptible bow of his head. There is no grand fanfare, no show of emotion—just the quiet recognition of the King's words.

Volk *(with quiet respect, his voice low and steady):*

"Mrhban."

The King nods in return, his own respect palpable in his greeting. There is a moment of silent understanding between the two men, a recognition of shared experience, though they occupy such different worlds.

King *(leaning forward slightly, his voice curious but also filled with admiration):*

"Your skill and bravery are admirable, and I've heard of your strength. Why live here, in this desolation, when men like you are needed in the royal guard? I extend my hand to you, with an invitation to join us."

Volk's eyes flicker to Yuki, who remains steadfast by his side, watching the guests with an unwavering gaze. The wolf's presence is imposing, yet somehow calming, as though it is as much a part of Volk as the air he breathes.

Volk *(after a long pause, his voice low and steady):*

"There is nothing out there for me. What I need is here, with my companions."

The King studies him for a moment, a flicker of curiosity passing through his eyes. He leans back slightly, absorbing Volk's words, then continues.

King:

"Why such solitude? Surely you have family, a past that calls to you."

Volk's gaze grows distant, the flickering flames casting shadows over his face as he looks into the fire, his expression darkening. For a moment, he seems lost in the weight of his own memories, as though they are too heavy to carry.

Volk *(with quiet finality, his voice low and rough):*

"The only family I know is here. I've made my peace with that. The people I cared for... are gone. Now these wolves and dogs are my family."

The King shifts slightly, his brow furrowing at the rawness of Volk's words. There is a brief flash of surprise in his eyes, but it's quickly replaced by understanding—perhaps even a touch of pity. He leans forward once more, his voice softer now.

King *(gently, as if searching for an answer):*

"What happened to you? Who were you before you came here?"

Volk's expression hardens, and the silence stretches out between them like a long shadow. His eyes narrow slightly as he recalls the fragments of his past—memories that are scattered, broken, almost lost in time. He doesn't immediately answer, and for a long moment, he seems consumed by the quiet of the room, the warmth of the fire, and the weight of his own past.

Finally, he speaks, his voice carrying the weight of unspoken pain. It is the first time the King has seen this man—this warrior—look so vulnerable. The flickering light from the fire casts dark shadows across his face as he begins to unravel the story that has defined him.

Volk *(in a low, gravelly voice):*

"I was a man of another time... another life. But that life is long gone. What I had, I lost... and what I have now, I've built from nothing but the will to survive. No family, no past... just the silence and the cold."

The King listens, his gaze softening as Volk's words hang in the air. There is no pity in his expression, only a deep understanding. In the harshness of Volk's life, in the solitude he has chosen, the King sees something familiar—a man defined not by the past, but by the strength he has found in his survival.

And in that moment, the space between them is bridged, not by titles or kingship, but by shared experience.

***

The harsh, unforgiving desert stretches out beneath a canopy of glittering stars. The air is dry, the night still, save for the quiet hum of distant winds. In the center of a modest tent, a young man, battered and bruised, lies unconscious on a cot. His body is a map of pain—deep cuts, burns and crude bandages, the result of brutal punishment, and the unforgiving nature of the life he's been through. Despite the harshness of his environment, his chest rises and falls with slow, steady breaths, a small but resilient pulse of life in the vast desert.

A *nurse* hurries around his cot, her hands shaky as she checks his vitals. She looks down at this man's still form, her eyes widening when she sees his eyelids flicker. She steps back quickly and calls out urgently.

Nurse *(anxiously, to the doctor):*

"Doctor! He's awake!"

The doctor enters the tent. A Russian man hardened by years of experience in this brutal profession, his face lined with age and wisdom that comes not from caring but surviving. His hands are quick and efficient, betraying no hint of tenderness, only practiced expertise. Behind him, a calm, focused *Arab man*, *Yousuf*, steps in, his gaze intense, observant, and inscrutable.

The doctor approaches, checking man's vitals as his eyes open slowly, bleary and confused. Man's vision swims, his surroundings unclear as his mind struggles to catch up with his body.

Doctor *(gruffly, trying to steady him):*

"Calm down. You're okay now."

But man's breath hitches. His pulse quickens, his eyes darting around the dimly lit tent, trying to make sense of the faces, the place, the pain. His voice cracks as he speaks, his words filled with fear and confusion.

Man *(hoarsely):*

"Who... who are you? Where am I? What's happening?"

The doctor exchanges a look with Yousuf, his expression grim. He turns away from the man for a moment, muttering something under his breath in Russian before speaking again.

Doctor *(muttering to Yousuf, low and steady):*

"As I suspected. The part of his brain tied to his memories... it's gone."

The doctor returns his focus to the man, his gaze hard but not unkind. He is a man used to dealing with the aftermath of violence, and this is just another form of it. He studies the man with detached interest as he tries again.

Doctor (calmly, but with the weight of authority):

"Look at me. What do you remember?"

The man's face contorts in pain as he struggles to grasp onto any memory, any piece of his past. But there's nothing. His mind is a blank slate, a vast, dark emptiness that only deepens with each passing second. Overwhelmed, man's eyes flutter shut again, his mind unable to process the chaos within him. His body falls limp as he slips back into unconsciousness, the weight of his own confusion too much to bear.

The doctor watches him for a moment, then turns toward Yousuf, his voice low but serious.

Doctor *(with finality):*

"He's lost everything. No memory. No past."

Yousuf steps closer, his gaze lingering on the man, the stillness of the moment not lost on him. He looks down at the unconscious man with a quiet respect, his lips twitching into the faintest of smiles.

Yousuf *(with a hint of admiration, his voice almost a whisper):*

"This desert consumes men whole. Only the brave swallow the desert. He's a lone wolf."

The doctor glances at Yousuf, a small, almost imperceptible nod acknowledging the truth of his words. But he remains focused on the task at hand.

Doctor *(dryly, to Yousuf):*

"A Volk?"

Yousuf's smile widens just slightly, as though he's made some subtle but important connection. The air is thick with unsaid words as the doctor and Yousuf exchange one last look over the unconscious figure of the man.

The night outside remains unchanged, the stars above cold and distant, just like the life that lies beyond these walls. But within this moment, a new chapter begins for Volk, one that he cannot remember, but one that will shape him into something far greater than the man he once was.

16 Months Later. The brutal desert sun beats down on a dusty training ground, the heat rising in shimmering waves from the sand. A group of *assassins* watches intently as *Volk* moves through his training regimen. Each strike, each movement is fluid and precise—almost as if he's not thinking, but *doing*. His body seems to be in perfect harmony with the weapons in his hands: a gun, a knife, and his bare hands. Every motion is calculated, executed with deadly intent.

Volk's focus never falters. He's calm, collected, his mind empty of anything but the task at hand. The constant rhythmic sound of his feet on the dirt is the only noise that breaks the silence. His face is a mask of concentration, emotionless and unwavering.

Yousuf stands in the shade, observing the scene with a calculating gaze. Beside him is *Mark*, a veteran assassin who has spent his life honing the art of killing with brutal efficiency. He watches Volk with the kind of detached admiration a craftsman might give to a perfectly sculpted tool.

Yousuf *(his voice low but filled with a certain pride):*

"Mark, I want you to train him personally. I've never seen such survival instincts."

Mark's eyes follow Volk as he disarms an opponent with startling speed and accuracy, his movements almost supernatural.

Mark *(gruff, with a nod of approval):*

"He's something else, alright. Focused. Trains like he's in a trance. In just six months, he's learned skills that take years."

Yousuf chuckles softly, crossing his arms with a sense of satisfaction that comes from seeing a creation unfold perfectly. His gaze remains fixed on Volk, the lone wolf in the making.

Yousuf *(with quiet admiration):*

"It's rare. A mind as clear as his. No past to haunt him, no thoughts to slow him down. A perfect weapon."

Mark turns his head slightly to glance at Yousuf, a slight grin tugging at the corner of his mouth. His approval is evident, though he remains a man of few words.

Mark *(with a wry smile):*

"You've got that right. A blank slate—unfettered by the usual baggage. Makes him a damn good killer."

Yousuf watches, his eyes narrowing with a quiet, knowing satisfaction. Volk's form is perfect, his technique flawless. The assassins around him look on with a mix of awe and wariness—Volk has quickly become one of them, but his absence of history, of personal conflict, makes him a creature of pure focus and efficiency.

As Volk completes his training, he stands still, drenched in sweat but showing no sign of fatigue. He turns, and his eyes meet Mark's for the briefest moment—a silent acknowledgment between mentor and pupil.

The desert sun continues to blaze down on the camp, but for Volk, the heat of the world outside is nothing compared to the fire that burns within him—a fire forged by his training, his mind, and his emptiness.

Years Later. The salty sea breeze whips through the air, carrying with it the weight of years spent in the shadows. *Mark* stands at the edge of the dock, his weathered face set in a solemn expression. A heavy bag hangs from his hand, the last vestige of a life he's leaving behind. He's no stranger to goodbyes, but this one feels different.

Beside him, *Volk* stands as motionless as a statue, his eyes scanning the horizon, though his mind is a thousand miles away. He's been through this moment countless times before, but this is different—it's the end of a chapter.

The small group of *assassins* watches silently from the shadows, each of them understanding the weight of the moment. There's no laughter, no fanfare. Just the quiet respect of men who've shared battles, blood, and secrets.

Mark turns to Volk, his eyes hard, but beneath the surface, there's something else—something almost like regret, or perhaps just a heavy sadness.

Mark *(his voice steady, almost reluctant):*

"Take care, Volk."

Volk's face is a mask, but his eyes betray something—a faint glimmer of emotion, carefully concealed beneath years of discipline.

Volk *(his voice low, sincere):*

"Take care, Mark."

For a moment, they stand there, as if the world has stopped just for them. Then, without another word, they clasp hands—an exchange of trust, of loyalty, of shared history. It's rare for Volk to show any sign of affection, but Mark has earned it. This bond is forged in the fires of their past, silent and unspoken, but undeniable.

Mark pulls away first, turning towards the awaiting boat, his footsteps steady but heavy. He doesn't look back, and Volk doesn't move to stop him.

As Mark walks away, Volk's gaze shifts, his attention drawn to the *Agent* standing in the distance, partially concealed behind crates. His eyes are sharp, calculating—an unfamiliar presence in this moment, yet one that Volk recognizes with a flicker of curiosity.

The Agent watches Volk intently, though his expression is unreadable. Their eyes meet for a brief instant—an exchange of silent recognition. The Agent's mission is clear, but Volk remains unmoved. There's nothing left for him here, and whatever the future holds, it's a path he'll walk alone.

Volk takes one last look at the port, at the water stretching endlessly before him, and then turns away, his purpose clear. He walks into the unknown, a lone wolf once more—his past fading behind him, but the future ever beckoning. The winds of destiny stir, and Volk is ready to face whatever comes next.

The Agent's gaze never wavers. The game is just beginning.

***

The fire crackles, its warmth dancing in the dimness, casting moving shadows that stretch across the rough-hewn walls. The steady glow bathes *Volk's* face, revealing a rare and fleeting softness, one that betrays the hardened exterior he's built over years of solitude and combat. His eyes flicker toward the King, searching for the right words—something he hasn't needed to do in years.

There's a brief hesitation before *Volk* speaks, his voice uncharacteristically low, almost as if he's revealing something he's never dared to put into words before. He avoids the King's gaze, his thoughts drifting to a past that has long haunted him.

Volk (softly, as if confessing to himself):

"When Mark decided to leave... it wasn't the same. I lost my only friend... my mentor."

Volk pauses, eyes darkening.

"And when that loneliness became too much, I asked Yousuf to let me go—to disappear somewhere far from all the blood and noise."

The King listens, his posture relaxed, but his eyes sharp and full of understanding. The weight of Volk's words settles in the air between them, like a heavy fog. The stoic expression on his face softens, and for the first time, the King's usual regal detachment gives way to something more genuine—empathy, born from the recognition of shared pain.

King *(his voice low, warm, heavy with sincerity):*

"So much to bear... so much to take. My friend, if you ever need anything, please allow me the honor of repaying my debt."

Volk's gaze finally meets the King's—steady, unreadable, but with an almost imperceptible flicker of something softer. A nod passes between them, simple but full of meaning. The exchange is silent, yet louder than any words could be. It's an acknowledgment of the weight they both carry, but also of the fragile bond that has begun to form between them in this quiet moment.

The fire pops once more, breaking the silence.

The King rises from his seat, his entourage following his lead. The respect in their eyes is palpable as they move toward the door, leaving Volk with his thoughts. The cabin's warmth lingers, though the growing cold outside soon begins to creep back in, reminding Volk of the solitude that awaits him once more.

As the door clicks shut behind the royal party, a lingering sense of reverence hangs in the air. The shadows of the cabin stretch longer now, reflecting the weight of the conversation, and Volk is left alone, once again, in the company of his memories.

But tonight, something is different. A door has been opened—whether by the King's words or by Volk's own rare confession, it's impossible to tell—but there is a shift, a subtle shift, in the unspoken narrative of this place. It's as if the silence no longer feels so absolute.

Moments later, Volk stands just outside his cabin, his loyal wolf, Yuki, at his side. Together, they watch as the King and his party make their way back to the helicopters, the cold night air filling with the sound of engines roaring to life.

The hum of the choppers grows louder, disturbing the stillness as snow flurries are kicked up, filling the air with a soft haze. Volk stands resolute, his figure silhouetted against the fading evening light. His gaze remains fixed on the helicopters as they lift off one by one, carrying the royal party back to the world he left behind.

The final chopper rises, and as it vanishes into the distance, silence once again descends over the cabin. Volk stands motionless, Yuki pressed close to his side. The day has almost surrendered to the night, leaving Volk alone with the vast, endless quiet of the Siberian wilderness.

After a long moment, Volk turns and, with a final glance at the horizon, steps back into his cabin, closing the door behind him. The fire's glow flickers through the window as the party look below.

Echoes from the Valley

The study exudes an aura of sophistication, with soft lighting accentuating the rich mahogany of the desk and the gleaming artifacts lining the shelves. A serene calm fills the space, but the quiet hum of Amelia's thoughts disrupts the stillness. She sits, alone at her desk, the glow from her laptop illuminating her face as her fingers absentmindedly twirl a pen. Her mind is elsewhere, wandering back to Ladakh—the stark landscapes, the spiritual stories, and the sweet figure of "Shiva" that Tashi had mentioned.

Amelia's gaze narrows, a subtle shift of curiosity flickering in her eyes. She exhales slowly, her resolve firming. With a steady hand, she opens her laptop and types into the Google search bar:

"Shiva, Kashmir."

She hits enter, her fingers slightly trembling as the screen floods with results—mostly generic, referencing Lord Shiva, or travel-related articles about Kashmir. Her eyes scan, frustrated, clicking through a few pages, but nothing reveals the answers she's seeking. She's about to close the laptop in disappointment when something catches her eye.

A LinkedIn profile.

Shiva - Alumni, Indian Institute of Foreign Trade, New Delhi.

Amelia's breath catches. Her pulse quickens as she clicks on the profile, heart hammering with a mix of excitement and uncertainty. The profile, long dormant and untouched for nearly a decade, seems innocuous at first—basic details, education, professional history. Yet there's a pull, a feeling of inevitability as she continues to read.

The more she scans, the more she feels the pieces falling into place. The name, the education at a prestigious institution, the silence of the years—it all feels eerily familiar. Could this be the same Shiva that Tashi spoke of? Could this be the elusive figure tied to Volk's past?

Her fingers hover over the keyboard, but she doesn't type. She scrolls, almost reverently, through the profile, carefully reading each detail, as if uncovering layers of a life hidden behind words. The "Recommendations" section draws her attention next. She clicks through the first one, and her brow furrows in concentration. The words from Shiva's past colleagues are warm, glowing with admiration. Descriptions of a man who was brilliant, resourceful, fiercely independent—and above all, reliable.

A strange sense of urgency builds inside her. She reads each recommendation, each word, absorbing the significance of these relationships, of the life that Shiva must have lived before he disappeared from LinkedIn. Where is he?

Intrigued beyond measure, Amelia opens the profiles of a few individuals who appear closest to him. She jots down names, making notes in her notebook as she reads, a plan beginning to form—but no clear direction yet. Just a growing hunger for answers, a desire to understand the man who has so clearly impacted Tashi's life, and perhaps Volk's as well.

Amelia leans back in her chair, staring at the screen as the weight of her findings settles over her. A sense of certainty rises within her—this Shiva could indeed be Volk, the same man she's heard about in fragmented whispers, the figure who lingers in the stories of those who have crossed paths with him. But the question now is: what is the connection between this man, the mysterious world he comes from, and the enigmatic wolf-like figure of Volk who haunts her thoughts?

Her hand tightens around the pen, the tip scratching anxiously across the paper. She's on the cusp of something, something significant. And this time, she's determined to uncover the truth.

***

Amelia's mind was still preoccupied with the search when she met Peter, a man in his sixties, at an upscale restaurant later that week. Peter, a well-known business analyst, exuded an air of quiet authority. His salt-and-pepper hair and sharp suit spoke of a man who had earned his place in the world. They sat across from each other at a corner table, the restaurant's elegant decor adding to the seriousness of their conversation.

Peter sipped his coffee slowly, eyeing Amelia with curiosity. She leaned forward slightly, her face calm but her eyes revealing the determination that drove her.

"I appreciate you meeting with me, Peter. I came across your recommendation for a man named Shiva from India," she said, her voice polite but purposeful.

"I have a friend who's lost contact with him, and I was hoping you might know something about his whereabouts."

Peter set his cup down with a sigh, as if the name had taken him back to a distant memory. He leaned back in his chair, gathering his thoughts.

"Shiva... now there's a name I haven't heard in a while," Peter said slowly.

"I met him only a couple of times, at business events in New Delhi and Dubai. The last time I saw him was around twelve years ago. The rest of our conversations were mostly digital. He was one of those rare people who valued relationships—even in the professional world."

Amelia nodded, prompting him to continue. She leaned in slightly, her focus entirely on the older man across from her.

"He was brilliant, no doubt."

Peter went on, his tone thoughtful.

"Sharp, insightful, always asking the right questions. A good man with a unique perspective. We'd exchange

ideas on strategy and market moves. I even sought his perspective a few times, which is rare for me."

He chuckled, a brief smile tugging at his lips.

Amelia's curiosity deepened.

"What was he like? Outside of work, I mean. Did he ever... share anything personal?"

Peter hesitated for a moment, his gaze drifting toward the window as he gathered his thoughts. A wistful smile spread across his face, but there was a hint of mystery in his eyes.

"Not really," he replied with a shrug.

"Shiva was an enigma. Some people found him inspiring; others found him... challenging. He had a way of pushing people's buttons, you know? If he thought you were too rigid, too set in your ways, he wouldn't hesitate to challenge you. But he was always respectful, always tactful. Honestly, I wish I knew more about him."

Amelia's brow furrowed slightly. She had hoped for something more concrete, something that would piece together the scattered fragments of Shiva's past, but it seemed that even those who knew him couldn't fully unravel his complexities. She thanked Peter and left the restaurant, her thoughts swirling as she processed the fragments of information.

The next few days were a blur of meetings and interviews. Amelia traveled from one location to the next, meeting a variety of people who had known Shiva over the years. Each encounter added a new layer to the mystery, but none of the pieces fit together in any meaningful way.

In a sleek office building, Amelia sat with a tall woman in a sharp suit, who spoke passionately about Shiva's vision.

"He was innovative, stubborn as hell," The woman said with a grin.

"But he saw things others didn't. That's what made him special."

In a hotel lobby, a balding man with a serious demeanor spoke dismissively.

"Shiva was always too intense. Always questioning everything. He never knew when to stop."

The words rang with the bitterness of someone who had been challenged, perhaps even uncomfortable, in Shiva's presence.

In a crowded cafe, a young entrepreneur beamed as he described Shiva's brilliance.

"He was a visionary, but he kept to himself. Very private. It's like he never really needed anyone."

And in a dimly lit office, an older gentleman spoke with nostalgia.

"He was a curious one. Never afraid to ask questions, even if it made people uncomfortable. You either liked him or hated him."

Each meeting was a fragment of a puzzle—shifting, contradictory, never quite complete. Amelia jotted down names, notes, and impressions, but the image of Shiva remained elusive, like a figure in a fog. He was admired, yes. Respected, even disliked by some. But who was he really? What drove him? What had happened to him all these years?

Frustration gnawed at Amelia as she stared at her notes. The pieces of Shiva's life just didn't seem to fit together. But she couldn't stop herself. The mystery tugged at her, urging her to dig deeper. She had to know who Shiva was and why he had vanished from the world.

With a determined breath, she wrote down one final name, her hand steady despite the growing sense of urgency. Maybe this person, this last lead, would finally give her the answers she sought but even this person was of no help.

The mystery of Shiva wasn't over yet. And Amelia was determined to uncover the truth.

Amelia sat at her desk, her fingers absently flipping through the pages of her notebook. The pages were filled with notes, names, and observations—fragments of conversations, hurriedly scribbled down in an attempt to piece together the mystery of Shiva. But despite her efforts, the puzzle remained incomplete. The more she uncovered, the more she felt as though she were running in circles. There was something impenetrable about him, a wall he'd erected around his true self that no one could breach.

Her gaze wandered to the world map pinned on the wall across from her, its edges frayed from years of use. The various places she had visited pinned, the cities that had shaped her life—she had seen so much, yet this man, this enigma, was one step ahead, always out of reach. As her eyes traced the map, she found herself lingering on one particular place:

Kashmir.

A spark of realization flickered in her mind. None of the people she had spoken to had known Shiva outside of his professional life. No one had mentioned his personal side, his motivations, or the parts of him that weren't tied to business. **Kashmir**—that was the one place where Shiva had been truly himself. She had to go there, she knew it now. If anyone held the key to understanding him, it would be in Kashmir, a place where he had once been more than just a figure in the business world.

She murmured softly to herself, her voice barely audible in the stillness of the room.

Amelia (murmuring to herself):

"If no one here knew the real Shiva... then maybe Kashmir holds the answers."

Her voice was calm, but a deep sense of resolve settled over her. She stood up, her reflection in the dim light of the window showing a woman no longer uncertain, but driven by a singular purpose. Amelia moved with determination, pulling her phone from her pocket. Her fingers moved quickly, making arrangements, confirming her flight.

In the quiet of the mansion, everything around her seemed to fade away as the weight of her decision settled in. She would leave everything behind and go to Kashmir. There, she would uncover the truth about Shiva, the man who had become an obsession. And perhaps, just perhaps, she would finally discover who he truly was.

The next day, Amelia stood at the bustling airport, the noise of travelers rushing past her barely registering. She stood still, her suitcase by her side, eyes locked on the printed photo of Shiva in her hand. He was looking directly at the camera, a faint smile on his face. It was the kind of smile that seemed familiar, as if she had seen it before, but there was something elusive about it—something she couldn't quite grasp. It was a smile that felt like a memory slipping through her fingers, always just out of reach.

Amelia's fingers tightened around the photo for a moment before she tucked it back into her bag, her gaze hardening with newfound determination. There was no turning back now. She had made the decision to chase the truth, wherever it would lead.

With one last glance at the airport, she squared her shoulders and moved toward her gate. The noise of the airport faded as her mind focused entirely on the journey ahead. She would go to Kashmir, to the place where Shiva had once lived and worked, to the place where, she hoped, the answers would finally be found.

As she boarded the plane, the seatbelt sign flickered on, and Amelia leaned back, closing her eyes for a brief moment. The aircraft began to taxi down the runway, and the roar of the engines filled her ears as the plane lifted off the ground. Her gaze turned toward the window, watching as the world below shrank away, leaving only the vast sky before her.

As the plane ascended into the clouds, Amelia's journey to uncover Shiva's truth was just beginning.

Kashmir. Amelia sat in the back seat of the sleek black Mercedes; her gaze fixed on the breathtaking scenery outside. The car glided through the snow-covered valleys, winding along narrow mountain paths. The peaks loomed like ancient sentinels, their white caps glistening in the sharp daylight. The peaceful landscape was in stark contrast to the whirlwind of thoughts in Amelia's mind, but she was determined. The journey had led her here, to this remote corner of the world. A place where the mysteries surrounding Shiva might finally come to light.

As the car descended toward a small village, Amelia couldn't help but notice the simplicity of the surroundings. The village, with a modest population of around five thousand people, felt like a forgotten pocket of the world. The streets were quiet, the air crisp and fresh, and the people moved with a calm pace that seemed to reflect the pace of time itself in this place.

Amelia stepped out of the car and began her search. She spoke to the local shopkeepers and villagers, all of them giving her the same direction: Shiva's home. Each conversation only deepened the mystery of this elusive man. None of the villagers seemed to know much about him, but they all spoke of him as a figure of importance.

She finally arrived at a small shop tucked between two houses, a modest wooden structure with faded signs. Inside, a man in his early forties sat behind the counter. His name was Faizan, and when Amelia pulled out the photograph of Shiva, his expression shifted immediately. His face softened as memories flooded him, and his eyes filled with emotion.

Amelia (softly):

"I guess you know him."

Faizaan (nodding slowly, his voice thick with nostalgia):

"Yes. He was my best friend."

Amelia's heart quickened. Finally, someone who knew Shiva, someone who had known him personally. She leaned forward, eager for answers.

Amelia:

"That's wonderful. I can't believe it. Where is he? Can I meet him?"

Faizan's face crumpled with grief, and the warmth in his eyes dimmed. The weight of his next words hung heavily in the air.

Faizaan (somberly, barely holding back tears):

"He's no more."

The words felt like a physical blow. The air around them seemed to thicken, the silence hanging like a cloud. Amelia's breath caught in her throat, her mind racing to process what she had just heard. Shiva—this man she had been chasing, this ghost from the past—was dead?

Inside the shop, Amelia and Faizaan sat across from each other, the translator positioned nearby. Amelia spoke in English, her words flowing with sincerity. Faizaan responded in his native accent, his voice heavy with the grief of a lost friend.

Amelia (gently, with compassion):

"I'm so sorry to hear that. In Siberia, we met a man with a tattoo that resembles Shiva's."

As the moment unfolded, Amelia recounted her encounter with Volk in Siberia, the enigmatic man whose memory seemed to be a blank slate, and the series of events that followed. She watched closely as Faizaan listened intently, his eyes narrowing slightly, processing every word she said.

Amelia:

"When we met him, Volk had no memory of his past. If he's Shiva, I was hoping to reconnect him with his life here."

Faizaan remained silent for a moment, a mix of sadness and pride playing across his face. When he spoke again, his words were firm, and his tone was resolute.

Faizaan (shaking his head, with a mix of sadness and pride):

"There is nothing about this man that would resemble Shiva. Shiva was a beautiful soul, someone who believed in peace and non-violence. He never even harmed an insect."

Faizaan recollected a memory, a vivid recollection of youth.

***

Two young boys, Shiva and Faizan, were riding their bicycles through the rugged wilderness of Kashmir. The path was narrow and winding, the mountains towering around them. Faizan, already an expert at navigating these trails, grinned at Shiva as he pedaled confidently ahead.

Faizaan (cheerfully):

"shiva, ma bar parawai, yi na chunnè kiheen. Mya chu yi waaryah latè kormut."("Shiva, don't worry! It's not difficult—I've done this so many times.")

Shiva (hesitantly, his voice filled with uncertainty):

"Faizaana, be ha chussei thazraas khoachaan." ("Faizan, I'm scared... I'm afraid of heights.")

Faizaan (reassuringly, with a teasing smile):

"Che chui na mei pyeth bharoasè? Walla, chyeair ha gaxchie!"

("Don't you trust me? Just come down, we're getting late.")

Shiva hesitated, gripping the brakes, his heart racing. He was always cautious, always measured. But Faizaan was persistent, urging him to take the leap. Slowly, Shiva let go of the brakes. His bike sped down a steep, narrow trail, the incline nearly vertical. His heart pounded in his chest, but he focused, trusting his instincts.

The wind rushed past him, the ground coming up fast. Shiva's face was tight with concentration, but he stayed in control. At the bottom, he finally reached a flat patch of ground, his heart still racing but the exhilaration washing over him.

Faizaan (grinning widely):

"Wuchtè? Wonmai na, yi ha chu basaan goade goade khatarnaak?" ("See? I told you—it only looks scary the first time.")

Shiva (breathing heavily, a wide grin on his face):

"allai, Yath ha chu mazzè balaai!"

("Ohh! That was fun!")

They hugged and jumped around with joy, the thrill of the moment consuming them. It was a small victory, but one that would stay with both of them for years to come.

As the sun began to dip below the horizon, casting long shadows across the valley, Shiva and Faizaan cycled their way home. The air was cool, the sky a soft orange hue as the day came to a close.

Faizaan (waving over his shoulder):

"nearsa yaara khodayas hawaal, teli samkhov pagah!"

("go home in god's protection, we'll meet tomorrow then")

Shiva nodded in acknowledgment but didn't respond, his mind already drifting back to the climb, the rush of the descent, and the wild sense of freedom he had felt high up on those craggy cliffs. Faizaan's carefree spirit was a constant pull, tempting Shiva to forget about the worries of his father, his studies, his future. But today, there was something different. Something nagging at the back of his mind, a sense of unease.

From the balcony of their home, Shiva's mother watched him approach. She had been waiting for him, as always, her gaze sharp and filled with concern. As he pushed the bike into the small yard, she stepped down the stairs to greet him.

Shiva's mother embraced him tightly, her arms warm and comforting but her expression betraying a trace of worry.

"Mei oasmai na wonmut sulli ha yizi?"

("I told you to come home early")

She said softly, the familiar note of concern threading through her voice.

"Moul ha aasi pakaan garrè kun!"

("Your father will be back soon.")

Shiva smiled, trying to push away the knot of guilt in his stomach.

"Hattai, mei kya kor! Be draas thoda nyebar taam chakras, beyi nei kiheen!"

("But what did i do, i went out for a little adventure outside, nothing else")

She pulled away slightly, looking him over with a mixture of affection and silent reprimand.

"chakras"

("Adventure...")

She murmured, her tone soft yet stern.

"dohai maa phyerakh watti watti. parun karun chui na cxe?"

("You can't wander off like that every day. don't you have to study?")

Shiva explained the entire incident to her excitedly.

Later that evening, Shiva's father arrived home. The polished Ambassador car rolled into the driveway, its sleek form gleaming under the fading light. He stepped out, his suit sharp and impeccably tailored, the picture of a respectable government officer. The steady clack of his shoes on the stone path echoed through the yard as he entered the house, his presence filling the small space with a quiet authority.

Shiva's mother, already in the kitchen, spoke to him as he changed his clothes, recounting her son's little mountain adventure. The pride in her voice was palpable, but there was something else there too, a shadow of unease that seemed to hang in the air.

Shiva's father paused, his back to her as he unbuttoned his jacket. His face hardened, a slight frown creasing his forehead. He didn't say anything for a long moment, and when he did, his words were slow, deliberate.

The next morning, Shiva sat at the breakfast table, the weight of the previous night's conversation still pressing on him. His father sat across from him, his posture stiff, his gaze steady. Shiva couldn't meet his eyes, staring instead at the plate in front of him.

His father's voice broke the silence, but there was an edge to it, a quiet expectation.

"padhaey kis chaey chalaan?"

("How are your studies going?")

Shiva hesitated before answering, his thoughts clouded by the weight of his father's gaze.

"theekhei cha"

("They're going fine,")

He replied, his voice quiet.

His father didn't miss a beat.

"magar choun math teacher hey ous mei badli daleel wanaan."

("But your maths teacher was telling me a different story about it.")

Shiva flinched, looking down at his food, a deep flush creeping up his neck. He hated this part—when his father's disappointment settled over him like a heavy fog.

"Math chu mye mushkiley pahan basaan."

("Math is just a little difficult for me,")

He muttered, barely audible.

His father's expression hardened.

"yeman pahadan khasan viz koun chaey mushkil gachxaan."

("And doing stunts in the mountains isn't?")

The room fell into an uncomfortable silence. Shiva shifted in his seat, his stomach churning with guilt and shame. His father's words stung more than he cared to admit, but there was something deeper: a feeling of letting his family down.

Shiva glanced at his mother. She met his gaze for a moment before looking away, her face a mixture of concern and gentle reproach.

"baba wan karnè dobaarè."

("Dad. I'll never do it again.")

"mye ous faizaan wanaan, natè gaxcha nè bè."

("It was Faizaan who asked me to do it, otherwise i wouldn't have.")

His father's eyes softened slightly, but no forgiveness yet. Instead, he placed a hand on Shiva's shoulder—firm, but not unkind.

"Shiva,"

He began, his voice quieter but heavy with meaning.

"cxè chukh nè tethyen gharan hyund. teman gai hishi katha, tim chè rozaan tè maraan ethai paeth. cxè chui wenè waryah taraqee karèn bronh. mye chu aaz taam sorei taeth khaetrè kormuth."

("you don't belong to such families. it's the same thing for them, they live and die the same way. You've got to prosper a lot ahead. i have staked everything for it till now.

"bè chus yazath daar afsar. lukan chu mye peth aitemaad. faizaan'un moul chu sharaeb."

("I'm a respected officer. People depend on me. And Faizaan's father... he's a drunk.")

The words cut through Shiva, but he stayed silent. His father's hand remained on his shoulder, the pressure of expectations heavy.

"cxe chui ye sorui bronh paknawun. mye badlaev chanè mujub zindagi panin. wan chaey chean vaer naav banavnech. bey chui sarnei havun soun ayaal katè pyeth kout wout. wan chui cxei taam."

("You must carry this forward. I changed life for you. Now you must go farther, make a name, show the world our family's journey. It's your turn.")

Shiva nodded, overwhelmed.

"baba mye deezè maefi, wan karnè zanh."

("Forgive me dad, I'll never do it again.")

His mother reached over and wrapped them both in her arms, her eyes wet with emotion.

"myon gobur,"

("My good boy,")

She murmured.

Shiva sat there, the warmth of his mother's embrace the only thing grounding him. But inside, he was already retreating. His father's words echoed in his mind. The weight of dreams, expectations, and identity pressed on his chest.

As Shiva walked to school, the heaviness of that morning followed him like a shadow. He could hear Faizaan's voice in his head—light, joyful, reckless. But not today.

Just outside the school gates, Faizaan caught up, grinning.

"ya shiva ya, raath aava chakras mazai kin na ?"

("Hey, Shiva! How was the thrill yesterday?")

Shiva didn't answer. He kept walking, his pace quickening.

Faizaan frowned, catching up.

"cxe kya daleel ?"

("Hey, what's wrong?")

Shiva didn't stop.

"faizan, mya na aezyè nè dobaar wanaan yim cheez karnas. natè karzè nè mye seeth kathei."

("Faizan, please don't ever make me do something like that again. Or I won't speak to you.")

Faizaan blinked, taken aback. Then his face softened, serious now.

"acha… magar, chè chukh na myoun yaar wentè ?"

("Okay... then are we friends again now?")

Shiva's lips curled into a small smile. The weight in his chest eased just a little.

"emm.. chè chukh mye wen te yaar."

("Yes... you're still my friend")

The two of them walked into class together, their friendship intact—at least for now—but Shiva felt a sense of distance settling between them. Not just with Faizan, but with everything. His father's voice echoed in his head, a reminder that he was meant for something greater, something beyond the mountains, beyond the thrills of adventure.

And yet, in the quiet part of his heart, Shiva wasn't so sure.

Years Later. The sun hung low, casting long shadows across the dirt road as Shiva stood at the edge of his family's village, his packed bags waiting beside the cab that would take him away. His heart was a mixture of excitement and apprehension, a whirlwind of emotions he could barely keep track of. His mother, tears glistening in her eyes, held him tightly, unwilling to let go. The familiar warmth of her embrace, the softness of her touch, were both comforting and suffocating in the moment.

"shiva mya chu cxe peth fakhar."

("I'm proud of you, Shiva,")

His father's voice cut through the haze of emotions. He stood tall beside them, his usual stoic expression softened by pride, his hand resting firmly on Shiva's shoulder.

"mehnat kar bey karzè panun naav buland college'as manz."

("Work hard and make your mark at college.")

Shiva smiled, trying to keep the emotions at bay.

“ma bar gham, bè emè jaldi wapas.”

(“Don’t worry, I’ll be back before you know it.”)

His words were light, meant to soothe both of them, but he knew they couldn’t calm the storm brewing in his chest.

His mother, sobbing quietly now, kissed his cheek.

“panun khayaal thevzè bey aezyem karaan dohai phone.”

(“Take care and call me every day.”)

The driver honked, and Shiva’s father gently patted his shoulder.

“pakvaez, wanè nyearov. cxyear gov.”

(“Alright, let’s go. It’s getting late.”)

Shiva gave one last look at his parents, his heart swelling with love and a bittersweet ache. As the car pulled away, he could see them standing there, waving. His mother’s face was streaked with tears, but there was pride in her eyes. His father stood strong, his face betraying a rare vulnerability as he watched his son drive away, a part of him unwilling to let go.

***

The lecture hall was spacious, filled with rows of students hunched over notebooks and laptops, diligently taking notes or casually typing away. The hum of murmured conversations settled as the class began. At the front of the room stood Professor Kumar, a seasoned academic with years of wisdom etched into the lines of his face and the silver threads in his beard. His eyes sparkled with a quiet intensity as he explained theories about global strategies, scribbling complex diagrams on the whiteboard for his students to digest.

Shiva sat towards the back of the room, his attention fixed on the professor, his mind absorbing every word, every nuance of the lecture. But something nagged at him. He could feel the unease in the air, as though the concepts being presented were too simplistic, too one-dimensional. He couldn't help himself.

"Professor, I think the strategy is subjective," Shiva's voice cut through the air, loud and confident, his words ringing with the clarity of someone who had already thought through the matter deeply.

Professor Kumar stopped mid-sentence, his hand freezing over the marker. He turned slowly, his eyes scanning the room with a raised eyebrow, surprised by the unexpected interruption. Silence fell over the lecture hall, the students' attention now fully on Shiva, their curiosity piqued by the boldness of the comment.

"Yes?", Professor Kumar asked, his voice curious, but tinged with the slightest bit of challenge.

Shiva stood up, his posture straight, his eyes sharp. His classmates, who had been absorbed in their own thoughts, now turned to watch him. There was an undeniable energy in his presence, a kind of self-assurance that made them pay attention.

"Professor, I believe the strategy you described is subjective in nature,"

Shiva continued, his tone calm but assertive.

"For instance, applying this approach in a region with political instability could be disastrous. The risks could outweigh any potential gains."

The professor paused, his initial shock fading into thoughtfulness. He stroked his beard, his gaze shifting from Shiva to the rest of the class, considering the young man's point with genuine interest.

After a moment, Professor Kumar nodded, his expression softening.

"Of course. And not only this, but every strategy is subjective to the market," he said, stepping away from the whiteboard. His voice grew animated as he addressed the class, the spark of intellectual engagement lighting up his features.

"You see, if you blindly follow a strategy without adapting it to context, there is little chance of success. Here at business school, we teach you time-tested strategies, but what to apply, and when to apply it—that is where your intelligence comes in. If success were as simple as following a formula, every business graduate would be wealthy and thriving."

He turned back to Shiva, nodding in appreciation.

"Thank you, Shiva, for reminding us that strategy requires not only knowledge but also insight."

Shiva gave a small, appreciative nod and sat back down, the weight of the moment settling around him. Across the aisle, a girl with bright eyes and a soft smile watched him with newfound interest. Shanaya, seated near the back, had been paying attention to the conversation, but now her gaze lingered on Shiva, intrigued by the confidence he had just displayed.

Days later, the setting had shifted to a cozy, upscale restaurant, its warm, ambient glow casting a soothing light over the intimate space. Shiva and Shanaya sat across from each other, the city lights shimmering in the distance, a soft reflection of the night's magic. The restaurant buzzed softly with the hum of other patrons, but in their little corner, the world seemed to slow down, focused solely on their conversation.

Shanaya laughed, her eyes sparkling with amusement as she leaned in slightly, intrigued by Shiva's earlier bravado.

"I can't believe tumne Professor Kumar ko us tarah tok diya,"

("I can't believe you stood up to Professor Kumar like that,")

She said, her voice full of genuine admiration.

"Kya tum hamesha itni bekhaufi se sawaal karte ho?"

("Do you always question authority so fearlessly?")

Shiva smiled, a quiet confidence in his demeanor.

"Aisa nahi hai. Bas jab mujhe lagta hai ki kuch sawaal karna zaroori hai, tab bolta hoon."

("Not exactly. I just speak up when I think something's worth challenging.")

"Kai baar sabse acche jawaab wahi hote hain jo mushkil sawaalon se milte hain."

("Sometimes, the best answers come from the questions we dare to ask.")

The words hung in the air for a moment, and Shanaya's gaze lingered on him. There was something magnetic about his presence, something in the way he spoke—calm, assured, yet open to the complexities of the world. She found herself drawn to him, her curiosity piqued not just by his intellect but by the energy he radiated.

They shared a laugh, the connection between them palpable. Their conversation flowed effortlessly from one topic to the next—career aspirations, dreams, family dynamics, philosophies on life, and the experiences that had shaped them. Each exchange brought them closer, the chemistry undeniable. The evening passed in a blur of laughter and shared moments, the conversation growing more personal, the connection deepening.

By the time they left, walking side by side into the cool evening air, it was clear that something more than just intellectual respect had blossomed between them. The sparks that had started as curiosity now burned with something far deeper, something both of them couldn't ignore.

Years had passed, and Shiva had transformed from the bright-eyed young man who left his village for college into a successful and well-respected figure in the corporate world. Now in his early 30s, he was everything his family had hoped for—and more.

His tailored suits, sharp and impeccably fitted, spoke volumes about his newfound wealth and status. The Audi he drove was sleek, fast, and stylish, a perfect reflection of the man he had become.

He lived in a luxurious villa on the outskirts of the city, the modern decor a testament to his taste and success. Every corner of his home spoke of the ambition that had fueled him, from the high-end furniture to the panoramic windows offering views of the sprawling city in the distance.

His life was a whirlwind of business meetings and travel. He attended high-profile conferences and boardrooms around the world—New York, London, Dubai. He negotiated deals, shook hands with powerful CEOs, and built his empire with a relentless drive. The long hours of work were paying off. Deals that seemed impossible were closing, and his reputation was growing.

But there was one constant, one person who had been there through it all: Shanaya. She was always by his side, her presence a calming force in his life. They had grown together, supporting each other, sharing victories and losses. She was his foundation, and as his life expanded into the fast-paced, high-stakes world of business, she remained his anchor.

***

Shiva was seated in a first-class cabin on a long-haul flight, his sleek business suit still perfectly pressed despite the hours he had spent on the move. The glow of his phone illuminated his tired face as his fingers moved quickly over the keys, responding to the message from Shanaya.

"Hey, don't worry. It's just a one-day event. I'll be back by tomorrow."

He stared at the words for a moment before pressing send, but his exhaustion remained. There was a dull ache behind his eyes, a reflection of the relentless pace he had set for himself. As much as he wanted to be with Shanaya, there was no denying the importance of this conference.

The flight was long, and though the cabin was quiet and comfortable, his mind was elsewhere, focused on the work waiting for him at the conference. Still, he couldn't ignore the little tug of guilt at leaving Shanaya behind as their wedding day approached.

Shanaya, on the other hand, was surrounded by the bustling energy of her family's home.

The air was thick with the sound of relatives chatting, the clatter of wedding preparations in full swing, and the scent of delicious Indian food cooking in the kitchen. But despite the celebration around her, Shanaya's thoughts kept drifting to Shiva.

She was dressed in a vibrant Indian suit, the intricate embroidery gleaming under the soft lighting of the room. Flowers adorned her hair, and her heart should have been full of excitement for the days ahead. But as she read Shiva's message, a small frown appeared on her face.

"But Shiva, the wedding is in just five days."

Her fingers hesitated as she typed the words, feeling the weight of the message before pressing send. The wedding was meant to be a celebration of their love, the day they had been looking forward to for months. And yet, there he was, going hundreds of miles away, busy with a business deal. She couldn't help but feel disappointed.

Shiva's phone buzzed, and his eyes flicked down to read her reply. A sense of unease settled in his chest as he read the words. She was upset.

He quickly typed back, trying to reassure her.

"It was important for all of us. I'm really sorry, but I couldn't miss this conference."

He stared at the screen for a moment, knowing the conversation wouldn't be easy. But he had promised his team he would be there. This was a major client, and if he wasn't present, they might lose out on a significant deal. As much as he wished he could be with Shanaya, this was something he had to do.

Shanaya was pacing now, her phone still in her hand as the wedding preparations continued around her. But she couldn't focus on anything else. She felt torn between the excitement of her wedding and the frustration of Shiva's absence.

"But we're on our wedding leave," she typed, her frustration rising.

"Why did they have to pull you in now? Isn't it against corporate policy?"

Her thumb hovered over the keyboard for a long moment, and then she pressed send. She could feel her emotions swirling—hurt, frustration, and a deep longing to have him by her side.

Shiva read her message, and the weight of her words hit him harder than he expected. He knew she was right to be upset. He'd promised they would have this time together, and yet here he was, breaking that promise for business. He took a deep breath and began typing a response, his fingers moving swiftly.

"Babe, it's crucial. Major clients are flying in, and I've been working with them for two years. If I'm there, we're more likely to close the deal. And besides, Jennifer promised me that if I attend this conference, she'll extend our holiday by 45 days. We'll have a peaceful honeymoon, I promise. Just one day, and it'll all be worth it."

He stared at the screen for a moment, hoping his words would ease her concerns, though he wasn't sure they would. But he had to try.

Shanaya read his reply and sighed, the tension in her shoulders easing a little but not completely gone. She wanted to be supportive, she knew how important this was for Shiva, but it still stung.

"I still don't like it," she typed, her fingers tapping lightly against the phone.

"I miss you. Couldn't I have come along?"

Her heart ached as she pressed send. She wanted to be there with him, to share this part of their journey together. But it seemed like work always came first.

Shiva's phone buzzed again, and this time, he knew it was his last chance to reassure her. The seat belt sign flickered on as the plane began its ascent, signaling the end of their conversation for now.

"I miss you too, baby. It's only a day, and I'll be back tomorrow evening. Don't worry, everything will be perfect."

He quickly typed out one last message, his fingers moving fast as the cabin crew began to prepare for takeoff.

"Alright, babe, I have to go offline now. I love you, and enjoy the celebrations. I'll be back before you even know it."

Shanaya's reply came almost instantly.

"Love you too, bye."

With a small smile, Shiva put his phone on flight mode and settled back into his seat, the soft hum of the plane's engines the only sound around him. He leaned back against the plush leather chair, letting out a breath he didn't realize he had been holding. Everything would be fine. He would return soon, and they would have their moment.

As the plane began to climb higher, Shiva watched as the city lights below disappeared into the distance. He felt content, hopeful even, unaware that the events unfolding around him would soon shift everything he thought he knew. The turbulence of the future lay ahead, but for now, all he could do was lean back and enjoy the calm before it all changed.

***

The courtyard of Shanaya's family home was alive with the sound of celebration. Music filled the air, blending with the laughter of family and friends gathered for the joyous occasion. The space was adorned with marigold garlands and strings of twinkling lights, casting a warm, golden glow over everything. Shanaya sat at the center, nestled on an embroidered cushion, surrounded by the loving faces of her closest friends and relatives. Her hands were covered in intricate henna designs, the dark red stains a mark of the occasion, each swirl and pattern a symbol of love and tradition.

Around her, a group of women sang traditional songs, their voices rising and falling in harmony, clapping along to the rhythm. Shanaya smiled shyly as she glanced down at her decorated hands. Her friends teased her gently, saying that the darkness of her mehndi would signify Shiva's deep love for her. Their words brought a soft blush to her cheeks, and she laughed, feeling the warmth of the moment, though there was a quiet unease in her heart, a flicker of something unspoken.

In a quieter corner of the courtyard, Shanaya's father stood, watching her with a bittersweet smile. His eyes, filled with pride, lingered on his daughter as she prepared to embark on a new chapter of her life. There was love in his gaze, but also a sense of loss, the realization that his little girl was growing up and stepping into a future that was no longer within his control. He stepped away from the noise of the celebration, his heart heavy with emotion, retreating to a more private space in the house.

His phone rang, slicing through his thoughts. He pulled it out, struggling to hear over the music and chatter.

"Bhaiyya, news on karo. Abhi ke abhi,"

("Brother, turn on the news. Right now,")

A voice said urgently.

Shanaya's father strained to hear, his brow furrowing.

"Hello, kya hua? Yaha bahut shor hai!"

("Hello, what happened? There's too much noise here!")

The voice on the other end was choked with emotion.

"Bhaiya, main samjha nahi sakta... bas, TV on karo."

("Brother, I can't explain... please, just turn on the TV.")

His heart skipped a beat. The sense of dread that settled over him was instant. He hung up quickly, his pulse quickening, and moved with purpose toward the living room. As he passed the guests, their eyes flickered over him, noting his anxious expression. The music, once lively and full of joy, seemed to fade as he reached the TV. His hands trembled slightly as he picked up the remote and switched the television on.

The screen blinked to life, flashing images of chaos. The words

“WAR BREAKS OUT BETWEEN ARAB COUNTRIES”

scrolled in bold letters at the bottom. The noise from the television seemed muffled in his ears, as if a veil had descended over the room. His fingers fumbled for the remote, switching to another channel, hoping for a different report, some sign that this wasn’t real.

But the news only grew worse. The anchor’s voice was calm, but the words carried the weight of devastation.

“Breaking news. An airbus bound for Iran has been struck by missiles amid the escalating conflict. Reports confirm no survivors. All passengers are feared dead.”

Shanaya’s father’s blood ran cold. His face drained of color as the words sank in, each syllable sinking deeper into his chest. His hands shook as he switched the channel again, desperately hoping it was a mistake. But the same report blared from every news station, the images flashing across the screen as if mocking him.

The reality hit him like a punch to the gut. This was the same plane. The plane Shiva was on.

Outside, Shanaya felt a shift in the air. A strange heaviness fell over the courtyard, a sudden quietness amidst the festivity. She noticed her father standing at the living room doorway, his face pale, his body tense with fear. There was something deeply wrong. Her heart began to race, instinctively knowing that something had changed.

She stood up, brushing past her friends, her movements slow and deliberate. Her legs felt heavy as she crossed the room, her gaze fixed on her father, whose eyes were locked on the television screen.

As she entered the living room, her eyes followed the direction of his gaze. The words on the TV echoed through the room, each syllable a brutal reminder of the truth she wasn't ready to accept.

"...No survivors. All passengers on the airbus to Iran from India are feared dead."

The words were like a weight crushing her chest. Time seemed to stop, the room spinning around her as the truth settled in. The air in her lungs froze. Her legs gave way beneath her, and she collapsed to the floor, her body limp, her mind refusing to process the horror unfolding before her.

Her family rushed to her side, calling her name, but their voices seemed far away, muffled by the overwhelming grief that flooded her senses. Shanaya remained unresponsive, lost in a world of pain that was too much to bear. She was unable to comprehend the loss, the devastating truth that had shattered her life in an instant.

The room fell silent, and the world seemed to stand still. The screen on the TV flickered, the words repeating, but they no longer mattered. Shanaya was gone—her spirit lost in the overwhelming sorrow that consumed her.

***

While Amelia was in Kashmir, on the other side, Ahmed comes to meet Yousuf. The vast, desolate desert stretched endlessly under the unrelenting blaze of the sun. The air shimmered with heat, and the ground beneath was cracked and dry. Ahmed stood among a group of bodyguards from the king's palace, their dark figures standing in sharp contrast to the brilliant desert landscape. Dust swirled around them as they spoke with Yousuf, draped in traditional Arab attire, his face partially covered by a keffiyeh.

Ahmed's voice cut through the silence, his tone low, serious, and filled with authority.

"Ṣāḥib as-Sumū yureed an yaʿrif ʿan hādhā al-Folk. Kayfa intahā bih al-maṭāf fī arāḍīkum?"

("His Excellency wants to know about this Volk. How did he end up in your territory?")

Yousuf, standing tall, bowed his head slightly in acknowledgment.

"Āsha Ṣāḥib as-Sumū."

("Long live His Excellency.")

He paused, his gaze drifting over the barren horizon, his expression becoming distant as his thoughts began to wander back to another time.

***

The desert, still under the light of the early morning, unfolded in front of Yousuf. A caravan of camels trudged across the sand, their slow movements stirring small clouds of dust in the still air. Yousuf, dressed in flowing white, his keffiyeh wrapped tightly around his head, peered through a pair of binoculars, scanning the vast emptiness.

Through the lenses, his eyes narrowed as he spotted a lone figure in the middle of nowhere, on his knees and surrounded by a pack of Arabian wolves. The man, bloodied and battered, was struggling to fight off the animals, his bare hands flailing in desperation as he fought for survival.

Yousuf muttered to himself, his voice filled with disbelief and concern.

"Mā hāda al-junūn?"

("What madness?")

He signaled to his caravan, and they altered their course toward the lone figure in the distance. As they drew closer, the sight became even more astonishing. The man, despite his injuries, had managed to fight off most of the pack. A few wolves lay dead nearby, their jaws broken, as if the man had wrenched them apart with his bare hands. The remaining wolves, sensing the approaching caravan, quickly fled into the desert.

Yousuf dismounted his camel and walked toward the injured man, who was barely conscious, his body drenched in sweat, covered in cuts and bite marks. His breaths were shallow, his face a grimace of pain. Yousuf knelt beside him, sprinkling water on the man's face and gently lifting his head to pour a little into his mouth. The man coughed, struggling to stay conscious, his eyes unfocused.

"Anta bi-amān al-ān."

("You're safe now.")

Yousuf murmured softly, his admiration evident despite the situation. He had seen many survive the harsh desert, but this man, battered and bloodied, was something else.

With great effort, Yousuf lifted the man onto a camel, securing him as best as he could for the long journey ahead. The bloodstains on the man's clothes stood out against the stark desert landscape, as the sun began to rise behind them, painting the sky in hues of orange and pink.

***

The world of Shiva unfolded like a sharp contrast to that of Volk. Shiva, dressed in a tailored suit, moved through the polished halls of a corporate office. His presence was commanding, his every word in meetings filled with authority as he made deals and negotiated his way through the world of business. His life was one of luxury—private jets, fine dining, and extravagant parties. He lived in a world where success was measured by wealth and power, and everything he touched turned to gold.

In stark contrast, Volk's life was a constant battle for survival. He fought against nature itself, enduring harsh conditions in the wilderness. His body bore the scars of countless struggles, and his face reflected the toll of a life lived on the edge. Where Shiva thrived in luxury, Volk found himself constantly wrestling with the elements, his every movement marked by the need to stay alive. His world was brutal, filled with hardship, but it had shaped him into someone who would never back down, no matter the odds.

The two men existed worlds apart.

Amelia stood in the Kashmir valley, the stunning landscape surrounding her. The snow-capped peaks loomed above, their majesty undisturbed by the quiet confusion within her. She smoked a cigarette, the smoke curling lazily into the air, her eyes scanning the horizon, though her thoughts were far from peaceful.

"No way... they're the same person"

Her voice, barely above a whisper, trembled with disbelief. On the other side, Ahmed walked away from Yousuf's camp, his steps purposeful, his mind lost in thought. The stark desert stretched around him, a reminder of the harshness of the world they all inhabited. But Amelia stood far removed from it all, in the cool, green beauty of Kashmir. The contrast between the two places was stark—one hot, dry, and unforgiving, the other lush and tranquil. Yet, something was brewing—a connection that neither Amelia nor anyone else could yet see fully.

Desert of the Dead

The dimly lit cabin of the airplane was quiet, save for the soft hum of the engines. Shiva, clad in a tailored suit, sat slumped in his seat, his noise-canceling headphones blocking out the world. His eyes were closed, and his body seemed to be at ease as the plane cruised through the skies.

A soft tap on his shoulder broke the calm. It was the air hostess, her polite smile barely visible as she leaned in closer.

"I'm really sorry, sir."

Shiva blinked slowly, groggily waking from his sleep.

"It's okay," he muttered, his voice thick with exhaustion.

"The captain has turned off the seat belt sign. You may take it off now. What would you like for your meal?", she asked.

Shiva shook his head, his gaze drifting back toward the window.

"I'm fine, just need a nap. I haven't slept, and I'd appreciate it if I'm not disturbed throughout the journey."

"Sure, sir. Thank you for flying with Air India."

He closed his eyes again, sinking back into the seat, trying to ignore the world and slip back into his much-needed rest.

"Please wake me up when we land," he added without opening his eyes.

"Of course, sir," she responded.

Moments later, the hum of the plane was suddenly interrupted by the captain's cracking voice over the intercom. There was a note of urgency in his words.

"Ladies and gentlemen, due to escalating tensions, we are rerouting our flight to the Israel Air Station. Please excuse us for this inconvenience. You may use the Wi-Fi onboard to communicate with your loved ones. Thank you for flying with Air India."

Shiva remained unbothered; his mind clouded with sleep as he rested. But that peace was shattered in an instant. The plane jolted violently, the shock of the explosion reverberating through his body. The air hostess, caught off guard, was thrown off her feet and disappeared from his view.

A missile had struck the plane, tearing through its rear and sending debris flying in all directions. The panic of passengers screaming for their lives mixed with the blaring of alarms. The lights blinked and oxygen masks dropped from overhead compartments. It was chaos.

Shiva's heart raced, his instincts instantly taking over. He reached for the oxygen mask and slipped it over his face, securing it tightly. The captain's voice came through, filled with panic.

"Mayday! Mayday! Mayday!"

The plane plummeted, the angle steep and terrifying. Shiva gripped his seat, trying to steady himself as everything around him began to spin out of control.

"Brace for impact!"

The captain shouted; his voice almost lost to the chaos.

The world went dark.

***

Back home, in India, Shanaya laid unconscious in a hospital room, completely shattered. News channels reported the tragic crash, each word a bitter reminder of the devastating loss.

"The government has been attempting to contact Arab authorities to locate the remains of the crashed plane. So far, the bodies of 227 people have been identified who fell from the air. No survivors."

The news anchor reported solemnly.

A map appeared on screen, pinpointing the crash site in a war-torn region.

"Even if anyone somehow survived the crash, they would not make it out of the desert. The war situation in the area makes any rescue attempt impossible."

The anchor continued, his voice carrying the weight of finality.

An animation played, showing the missile's impact on the plane and the destructive path it followed, illustrating how the aircraft was doomed the moment the missile struck.

***

The explosion as the plane hit the desert was deafening, flames swallowing the sky in a fiery descent.

Shiva woke with a jolt, his lungs burning from the thick, acrid smoke. He gasped for air, his body on fire. He could feel the heat from his coat, the material scorched and smoldering. Pain shot through his shoulder, sharp and unbearable, as something metallic was lodged deeply within. Images of Shanaya, waiting for him at their wedding, flashed through his mind, pushing him to survive.

With what little strength he had left, he unbuckled his seat belt and tried to crawl from the wreckage. But as he moved, his head struck a seat, and everything went black again.

When he came to senses again, smoke filled the air around him. His vision was hazy, and pain coursed through his body. He fought to stay conscious, gritting his teeth as he pushed himself forward. Each step was a battle, but the urge to live kept him going.

He staggered a few meters away from the wreckage, but another explosion erupted behind him. The heat singed the back of his clothes as he collapsed onto the sand, unable to move.

Shiva's body was broken, battered, and burned from the harsh elements. His skin, once smooth and unscarred, was now raw and blistered from the scorching sun. The intense heat beat down on him relentlessly, unbearable in its force. His muscles ached with every step, his throat dry, and his vision blurred from exhaustion. But despite the overwhelming pain, he continued to walk, though each step felt heavier than the last. His legs wobbled, his knees buckling, and his mind struggled to remain conscious as the blistering desert sun continued to drain his strength.

The days blurred into one another; their passages marked only by the relentless rhythm of his stumbling feet. As the sun set, the coolness of the night brought no relief. The desert's cold bite settled deep into his bones. With every passing hour, his body deteriorated further. Yet, despite everything, something within him—something deep and primal—refused to surrender. He held on, clinging to the image of Shanaya waiting for him, the life they had planned together. That image was all he had left. It was his anchor, the only thing that kept him moving forward, even when his strength seemed all but gone.

The desert morning light bathed the sand in soft hues of gold, as if the sun itself was trying to soothe the harshness of the desert. But there was nothing soft about Shiva's situation. His body lay crumpled on the hot, unforgiving sand, unconscious, completely at the mercy of the desert. The sand beneath him offered a strange sense of calm, while the sand piling over him settled like a heavy blanket—harsh, yet natural, as if the desert itself had claimed him.

Around him, the wolves were watching. A pack of Arabian wolves, their sleek fur blending with the sandy dunes, circled cautiously. Their amber eyes gleamed in the early morning light, sharp and calculating, sizing up the man who lay before them. The leader, a massive alpha with dark fur, kept his gaze fixed on Shiva's still form, his nostrils flaring as he sniffed the air. The wolves' growls were low and resonant, as if they were deciding whether to approach or simply observe. The wind picked up, rustling the sand, and for a moment, the world seemed to stand still. Shiva, unaware of the danger around him, remained unconscious, his body an easy target for the predators.

Far off, in the same desert, Yousuf peered through binoculars, his eyes narrowing as he spotted something in the distance. His concern deepened as he muttered to himself.

"Ma hathihi al-junoon?"

("What madness?")

He said, a frown tugging at his lips.

***

Shiva was no longer alone. He was now lying across the back of a camel, his body limp, unconscious. His breathing was shallow, and the heat from the desert had sapped him of his strength. Yousuf and his men had found him and were carrying him through the vast expanse of the desert. The caravan of camels moved steadily across the desert, their long, slow strides cutting through the sand. The sun dipped below the horizon, casting a rich orange and purple hue across the sky. Long shadows stretched across the sand, the last remnants of daylight slowly fading away. The caravan of camels moved steadily forward; their silhouettes outlined by the fading light of the sunset.

***

Presently, far away, Volk is gliding effortlessly across a frozen lake in Siberia, the sled he rides pulled by a team of powerful huskies. Yuki, the lead wolf, races through the snow with purpose, followed closely by Zeus. The cold air nips at their faces, but they move with unwavering determination. The frozen beauty of the landscape stood in stark contrast to the storm of violence and chaos that had marked Volk's life.

To be Continued….